The Mystery of the Missing Ming

A Daisy Diamond Detective Novel

Cindy Vincent

Cinderov Books

Houston   Bozeman

The Mystery of the Missing Ming

A Daisy Diamond Detective Novel

Published by Cinderov Books
A Division of Mysteries by Vincent, LLC
For information, please contact:
Cinderov Books
PMB 373
1627 West Main Street
Bozeman, MT 59715

ISBN: 1-932169-37-7

Also by Cindy Vincent: Makeover for Murder, A Kate Bundeen Mystery

Printed in the United States of America

Dedication

To my childhood chums, Cheri, Nancy and Gary.
Thanks for adding so much fun to my younger years.

And to my husband, Rob, who invites the little kid in
me to come out to play.

And to Aunt Jean Hixson, great female flyer, member
of the Mercury 13, and excellent educator, who
encouraged all to excel in Math and Science.

CHAPTER 1

"Daisy Diamond, you really are the greatest girl detective of all time!" I smiled at my best friend as she crawled out from under my huge laboratory table.

She brushed the cobwebs from her long, dark hair and handed me my shoe. "I don't think finding your missing tennis shoe counts as real detective work."

"Maybe not to you, but I've been searching for that shoe for an hour."

Wowser! Was I ever glad to see that tennis shoe again. For a while I thought it was gone for good. That meant I would have to go through the rest of the school year wearing only one tennis shoe. Mom surely wasn't going to buy me another pair. Especially since I'd already ruined several pairs this year from my science experiments.

Daisy grinned at me. "Your shoe was easy to find. That's because you left a whole trail of clues."

"Huh? I didn't leave any clues." I, Sally Sosmart, girl scientist and inventor, may do many things, like invent stuff and create new gadgets to help people. But I do not leave clues.

"Sure you did. Everybody does." Daisy pointed to the door of my huge bedroom, which also doubled as my laboratory. "I've seen you walk through that door a million times. You always kick off your shoes the same way."

"I do?" I had no idea. I guess I'd never really paid attention before.

"Uh-huh. First you untie your left shoe. Then you toss it at a forty-five degree angle to the left of your body. Then you untie your right shoe and toss it to the right side of your body. Also at a forty-five degree angle."

"Okay, fine. So I'm a creature of habit." I pulled my golden-brown hair into a ponytail. Just like I always did. I guess I'd never noticed that before, either. But you can bet Daisy did.

"Most people are creatures of habit." Daisy started taking toe-to-toe steps across the polished wood floor of my room. "To find your right shoe, I simply asked you where you found the left shoe. When you told me that, I knew your right shoe should be at a ninety-degree angle from the left one."

"All right. I can do the math. Forty-five plus forty-five equals ninety degrees."

She stopped and made a quick turn. "That

meant your right shoe landed somewhere under your laboratory table." She pointed toward the table.

"But there's tons of stuff under there. How did you spot it? I didn't see it."

She grinned again. "When the shoe slid beneath the table, it left a disturbance in the dust."

"Huh? A disturbance? What do you mean by that?" I looked at my friend cock-eyed. I figured this must be one of those police words she'd learned from her dad. He was a detective for the Pinecrest Police Department before he and Daisy's mom went missing in the Amazon.

Daisy kneeled down and looked under my lab table. "It's like this," she said. "Dust usually settles in a smooth layer. So when something moves through it, or disturbs it, it leaves tracks. Kind of like footprints in the snow. The trail through the dust is called a disturbance."

"Oh, I get it."

Now she pointed beneath the table. "Of course, I noticed the disturbance in the dust right away. But I still couldn't see the shoe, since it must have knocked over a stack of notebooks when it slid toward the wall."

"So how did you finally find it?"

"The scent of geraniums."

"Huh?" Sometimes I wasn't sure if my friend was on the same planet that I was on.

"Yup, geraniums. Remember the last time you wore those shoes? That's when you tripped through your mom's geranium garden. Geraniums have a really strong smell, so some of the scent would have rubbed off on your shoes. So I just used my nose and followed the scent of geraniums. That's when I found your shoe under those notebooks that are under your lab table."

"Wowser," was all I could say. My friend Daisy was amazing. She knew exactly how to organize clues in a case to solve a mystery. She always said it was a lot like putting the pieces of a puzzle together. And she should know! After all, she had nabbed all kinds of criminals, from dognappers to cat burglars.

She looked around the room. "Maybe if you cleaned your room once in a while, it might be easier to find things."

I rolled my eyes and flopped onto my bed, hoping I wouldn't hear the same lecture I'd heard a zillion times from her. I hated the "Organize Your Room" speech. Even though Daisy and I were best friends and the smartest girls in our class at Pinecrest School, in some ways we were very different.

Daisy Diamond, super sleuth, liked everything to be neat and in its place. In fact, she could spot something that was out of place from a million miles away. That was just one of the reasons why she was such a great girl gumshoe.

But me, Sally Sosmart, scientist and great girl inventor, could care less about things being organized. In fact, I even liked my room to be a little cluttered.

Okay, wait, maybe that wasn't totally true. I didn't mind if my desk had stacks of things on top of other stacks of things on top of other stacks of things. And I didn't mind if it all looked like it could topple at any minute. I didn't care if every inch of my room was cluttered with junk of every color in the rainbow. It didn't bother me that my closet looked like an overgrown Venus flytrap that wanted to eat my backpack whenever I opened it.

Even so, whenever I worked on a new invention, I liked my working area to be neat and clean. I liked all my tools and materials to be kind of organized, so I could find stuff when I needed it.

But when it came to housework, as far as I was concerned, I had better things to do. My inventions were the most important things in the world to me. Well, except for my friends. And my mom and dad. And my little brother, Scare'em Aaron.

Okay, maybe my little brother wasn't really that high on my list of *Things That Matter Most to Me*. Sometimes I actually thought he was pretty cute for a little kid. Other times I wished he would run off and join the circus.

I sat up on my bed and glanced at Daisy. She was looking at my latest invention on my laboratory table. I could hardly believe she hadn't given me her usual speech about making my room squeaky clean.

I waved to get her attention. "Hey? What happened to the regular lecture?"

She straightened a stack of books and a smile slid across her face. "You know, if you picked things up around here, your mom would let you have a cat. She said you could have one if you cleaned your room and kept it that way."

Okay, I asked for it. And I got it, all right. Yup, this time Daisy hit home. She knew I'd been begging my mom for a cat for months now. Unfortunately,

Mom and I were stalled when it came to agreeing on the terms and conditions of getting a cat. Basically, it boiled down to this — I had to meet Mom's terms, or a cat would not be allowed to live under our roof . . . under any condition. I had been looking for a loophole in this deal, but so far, I hadn't been able to find one.

"I'm still working on my mom," I told Daisy while I tied my shoe. "I haven't given up on her yet."

Daisy picked up my latest invention, which, to the untrained eye, looked like a small black camera. "I'm just dying to know what this is," she said.

"I call it a WREB. And I'm dying to tell you all about it," I said in return.

Okay, that was an understatement. I was pretty proud of my new creation. I had worked very hard to invent it, and I had to figure out a lot of things to make it work.

Before I could tell her about my new invention, my watch began to sing, "Hello, Sally. It is twenty minutes until noon. Time to leave. You don't want to keep Hannah waiting."

I smiled and turned off the singing alarm of the big pink and silver watch. I built the watch last week and programmed the alarm to sound like my favorite boy band singer. The watch turned out to be pretty awesome, if you ask me.

Daisy put on her jacket. "Can we bring your new WREB with us in the car?"

"Sure." I jumped up from my bed. "I'll explain what it does on the way to Hannah's house."

"Good plan," Daisy said. "Otherwise we'll be

late."

She grabbed my new gadget and put it in the pocket of her jacket. I grabbed my own jacket and the book that my Aunt Melvinia wanted Hannah to have.

Then we were off. We raced down the long hallway of the second story of my house.

First we were going to have lunch with our friend, Hannah Hystory. After lunch at her house, we were headed to my Aunt Melvinia's old mansion.

You see, my Aunt Melvinia had just passed away and everything in her house was about to go up for auction. And believe me, that was a lot of stuff. But before everything was sold, Mom and Dad told me I could go to her house and pick out one item as a keepsake. You know, something to remember her by.

Holy Cannoli! That was a pretty tall order, if you ask me. How in the world was I ever going to pick just one item? To top it off, I felt a little funny about the whole situation. Me, going into her home, and looking through all her stuff. Some of that stuff must have been really important to her, or she wouldn't have kept it all. Kind of like my inventions are important to me.

It didn't help matters that I honestly didn't know her that well. She wasn't really my aunt. She was actually a distant relative on my dad's side. And for the last few years, she had just stayed inside that huge mansion of hers. She didn't want to go anywhere or see a lot of people. She was really old when she died, and I was sad when Mom told me the news. I couldn't help but think I had missed out on something.

And now I had to pick one item and only one item to remind me of her always. I had no idea what to choose, and today was the last day when I could pick a keepsake. After today, the house and everything in it would be turned over to the auction company. Then they would sell all the stuff at a really big auction.

So that meant I had to pick my one and only item this afternoon. How would I ever figure out what to take?

That's where Hannah came in. Hannah loved history. She knew all about old things and antiques. I was hoping that she and Daisy could help me figure out what item to choose.

Besides that, it's always good to have your friends with you for moral support.

I smiled at Daisy before we practically flew down the marble stairs to the first floor of my house. Well, actually, my house is more like a mansion, too. It's some old place that my father inherited from his father, who inherited it from his father. Anyway, the place is just a little too fancy for my tastes, and it's huge. I'm not crazy about huge homes. But the size can be nice when I'm trying to avoid my brother, Scare'em Aaron.

Luckily, he was nowhere in sight when Daisy and I zoomed through the front entryway and stopped at the front door. Our family chauffeur, Holmes, was there waiting for us.

Okay, I'll admit it. I'm kind of a rich kid. But I hate it when anybody calls me that, because I'm not a spoiled rotten little brat or anything. Mom doesn't buy me all the things I ask for, and I've got rules just like any other girl. Plus, my mom and dad don't go around with their noses in the air just because they've got a few dollars in the bank.

As for Holmes, well, my dad hired him because he was down on his luck and needed a job really bad. Now he's like part of the family.

Holmes smiled and bowed to us. "Good morning, Ms. Sally and Ms. Daisy. I trust you're ready to be taken to your lunch appointment."

As usual, his dark suit looked like he had been ironing it all morning. There wasn't a wrinkle on it. Every gray hair on his head was exactly where it was supposed to be and his mustache curled up like the handlebars on a bike. He carried his violin in its case, just like he always did.

I guess Holmes must be a creature of habit, too.

"Thanks, Holmes," I told him. "We're all ready to go."

"Very good, Ms. Sally. Please follow me then."

We followed him out the front door and down the cement steps. The sun was a bright yellow ball in the wide blue sky. A little breeze made the pine trees sway and make whispering sounds. I love the way pine trees smell. Last year I made some pine tree perfume for all my friends for Christmas.

Our navy blue car was waiting in the huge circular driveway. Holmes held the door for Daisy and me as we climbed into the backseat. Then he shut our door and went around to the front of the car.

Holmes climbed into the driver's seat, and put his

violin case on the seat beside him. He always brought his violin with him. He loved to play classical music, and it gave him something to do while he was waiting for us.

Daisy grinned at me. "Who knows," she said, "maybe we'll come across a new mystery today." She began to toy with the beads of the bracelet that she always wore on her left wrist.

Let me tell you about that bracelet. It's got some round beads, some diamond-shaped beads, and some daisy-shaped beads. The colors are beautiful. Blue, pink, teal and silver. Daisy's doctor mom gave it to her just before she and Daisy's father disappeared in the Amazon.

Daisy wears it every day. Talk about creatures of habit. And it seems like whenever she's about to find a really big clue in a very tough case, she starts to play with the beads on her bracelet.

Just like she was doing right now.

I rolled my eyes at her. "Don't even think about finding a new mystery today."

Her brown eyes sparkled. "Too late," she said. "I already did. Think about it, that is."

"Oh, no. That means it's only a matter of time before one pops up. Here we go again."

I looked at my big pink and silver watch. "I'd better set my alarm so I'll make it home on time."

"Why?" she asked, ever so innocently.

"Because," I told her. "You know how we can get wrapped up in one of these mysteries. Last time I got home late and my mom grounded me for a week."

"But it was for a good cause," Daisy protested.

"The lady who got her dog back was sure happy."

"I'm glad she was happy. Because my mom sure wasn't."

Daisy grinned while I set my alarm for five o'clock. My mom had told me to leave for home by six o'clock, or I'd be late for dinner. I figured if my alarm gave me a reminder at five o'clock, I could easily be on my way home before six. I didn't want to risk getting grounded again.

"There." I patted my watch. "That should take care of things."

Okay, maybe I was complaining a little. But the truth is, I was only kidding. I didn't really mean it. That's because I've had lots of great adventures with Daisy and her capers. And I'm sure we'll have many more.

I looked at Daisy's wrist, and the way she kept toying with that beaded bracelet. The people who know Daisy best have a saying about the great girl gumshoe.

Wherever Daisy Diamond goes, a mystery is sure to follow.

CHAPTER 2

Holmes started the engine and then looked in his rearview mirror to see us in the backseat. "Are your seatbelts properly fastened, ladies?"

I glanced at Daisy and she tapped the buckle of her shoulder strap. "All snug as a bug," I told him.

"Very well, then," he said. "We shall proceed to Ms. Hannah Hystory's house." He put the car in gear and drove it out of our circle driveway. He turned the radio on and tuned it to a station that was playing violin music.

Holmes was great. Not only was he a terrific driver, but he always watched out for us kids whenever we went somewhere. And believe me, that wasn't always easy, especially when it came to my brother, Scare'em Aaron.

I looked out the car window for a minute and watched fields of pink and purple wildflowers pass by. Then I remembered my latest invention.

I pointed to Daisy's pocket where she had stashed it. "So, are you ready to learn all about my new WREB?"

"Absolutely." She pulled out the little black box. "Okay," she said with her usual grin. "What does this thing do?"

"It's a cross between a camera, a microscope and a computer program that enhances images."

Whenever I talked about something I had invented, I always felt this tingling sensation across my skin. Kind of like goose bumps. I felt a lot like I did when I got a special present on my birthday. Only, it was much, much better than that.

Daisy looked through the small, round eyepiece on my WREB. "Hmmm . . . It looks just like an ordinary camera."

"I know. But it's different. It's actually a Word Restoration Box, or WREB, for short. I can use it to read words that have been damaged somehow and are too fuzzy to read anymore."

"Hmmm . . ." Daisy said. "Interesting. But when would you use it?"

I felt a smile cross my lips. "Okay, here's a good example. Do you still have that map we used when we went hiking in Big Pine Forest last weekend? You know, the map that got scorched in the campfire?"

Daisy nodded. "Uh-huh. Lucky for us, we remembered those broken trees on the trail to use for landmarks. Otherwise, we never would've found our way home after the map was ruined."

She dug into the pocket of her jacket and pulled out the folded and slightly browned map. She handed it to me.

"Thanks to my WREB, we'll never have to worry about something like that again." I spread the map out across the backseat of the car. Most of the map had been darkened from being too close to the campfire. I found the part with the worst damage and pointed to it.

"Look right here," I said. "You can't read the words on this part anymore, right?"

Daisy nodded her head. "Right."

I pushed a few buttons on my WREB and heard it make a quiet whirring sound. Music to my ears. It told me my invention was working and ready to go.

"Okay," I said. "Now look at the map through my WREB."

She held the box over the map and peeked through the eyepiece. A few seconds later, she made a noise that sounded like a cross between a gasp and a scream. She looked up at me with wide eyes.

"That's amazing!" she said. "I can read every word! It's like it was never damaged at all!"

"Uh-huh." I felt the smile on my face grow even bigger. Pride swelled up inside me, making me feel like I could float all the way to Hannah's house. Sure, maybe I did have the messiest room on the planet. And maybe I didn't always try to get along with my little brother.

But I could create things that other kids hadn't

even tried to invent. I guess you could say that inventing things was my special talent.

And most important of all, inventing stuff made me happy.

I picked up my WREB and looked it over. "My mom is getting a patent on this for me. Just like my other inventions."

Daisy's dark eyebrows crinkled on her forehead. "Hmmm . . . a patent. Your mom explained that to us once. That's when you fill out some forms and send a bunch of papers to the government. Then they give your invention a number and record everything in your name. So no one else can steal your invention. Right?"

I put the WREB in my pocket. "That's what my mom told me. Then I can make my invention and sell it as much as I want to. Or, I can give someone else permission to make it and sell it. I'll get that all figured out later. Someday, I hope my WREB will go up in the Space Shuttle. The astronauts could use it if they damaged any of their maps or books."

"Wow! Great idea." Daisy grinned. "I just know it will get there!"

I smiled back at her. Not only is Daisy the greatest girl detective ever, but she is also the greatest best friend, too. She always supports me on all my inventions, and she's honestly happy whenever I succeed at something. She's never been the envious type. In fact, if my WREB ever went up on the Space Shuttle, she would be cheering louder than anybody.

Wowser! As a girl scientist, I think the Space Shuttle is just the ultimate! I can't imagine anything more awesome than having one of my inventions go up on a mission. Except, that is, unless I got to go up on the Shuttle *with* my invention.

"Excuse me, ladies," Holmes said from the front seat. "We have arrived at Ms. Hannah Hystory's house."

Holmes pulled carefully along the curb. Daisy and I looked out the window to see Hannah's house.

Holy Cannoli, what a place! It was a huge home, and to me, it looked like a giant gingerbread house. The first time I had visited, Hannah's mom and dad told me it was a Victorian home. That meant it was built over a hundred years ago when Queen Victoria ruled England. I wondered if Queen Victoria made people build beautiful houses when she was queen. Maybe it worked so well in England that she got people in this country to do the same!

Hannah waved at us from the front door as Holmes let us out of the car. Today she was wearing one of her favorite outfits. It was a yellow dress with a wide, full skirt that had been made in the 1950s. Hannah collected old clothes, and she especially liked to wear clothes from the 1930s, 1940s or the 1950s.

"Lunch is ready, girls," she hollered to us. "And, boy, oh boy, does it ever smell good!" In the sunlight, her hair looked like the color of brand new pennies. "You can join us if you want to, Holmes. Mom made plenty and she said to be sure to invite you, too."

Holmes bowed to Hannah when we all reached the front steps. "Thank-you, Ms. Hannah, but I have already dined. Besides, I am on a very strict diet. I will wait for you ladies in the front room, thank-you."

Hannah held the door open wide and let us in.

Wowser! I always loved to step inside Hannah's house. It was just like going back in time. The house was full of really old furniture. The couches had humped backs, kind of like a camel's back, that were made of polished wood. The lamps were made of brass and the lampshades were decorated with fringe. The black and white pictures on the wall showed ladies in long dresses and large hats. An old Persian carpet lay across the polished wood floor.

Hannah's parents were antique dealers and Hannah loved old things as much as they did. In fact, Hannah loved old stuff as much as I loved inventing things. And as much as Daisy loved to solve mysteries.

Hannah showed Holmes to the parlor where he could wait for us. "Just make yourself comfortable," she told him. "That's Mom and Dad's most favorite piece of furniture in this room. They always have their guests sit on it. It's the most wonderful old sofa they ever found."

Holmes smoothed out his suit jacket and sat down. "Thank-you, Ms. Hannah. I shall enjoy my moments on this delightful furniture. Your hospitality is simply splendid." He'd brought his violin with him and he took it out of the case.

"Thank-you, Holmes," Hannah said before she turned to Daisy and me. "Hey, girls! Let's hurry up and eat so we can get to Aunt Melvinia's house." She took us by the hands and practically pulled us to the dining room. "I can hardly wait to get a good look at all the stuff inside. My parents are going to the auction next week. I'm sure I'll get to go with them. I can tell them what they should bid on. Besides that, they're going to need help packing up all the stuff they buy."

I ran along to keep up with her. "I think a lot of people are going to that auction."

"It'll be a very interesting day," Daisy added with a grin. "Just like I have a feeling today will be."

I glanced at her for a moment. I could almost see the gears turning inside her head. I wondered what she was thinking.

"I'll bet you're right," Hannah said just as we entered the dining room. "I can hardly wait to get going. Oh, by the way, Mom left us lasagna for lunch. I hope you like it."

"We love lasagna!" Daisy and I practically shouted at the same time.

I suddenly noticed the wonderful aroma in the air. Hannah was right. Lunch did smell good!

I heard Holmes playing his violin in the parlor as we took our seats at the old dining room table. The backs of the chairs looked like someone had carved them in the shapes of shields. Whoever made those chairs must have spent absolutely ages carving them!

Right above our heads was the most beautiful chandelier I've ever seen! It had lots and lots of strips of glass dangling from it. The whole thing sparkled in the sunlight and made rainbows dance on the table. Someday, when I was grown up, I wanted to have a chandelier just like it in my own house!

We dropped our napkins across our laps and started to eat. The lasagna was delicious. After two bites, I remembered the old book I'd brought for Hannah.

I pulled it from my jacket pocket and handed it to her. "Here's the book I told you about. I'm not sure what's in it. But my Aunt Melvinia told my dad that he absolutely had to give this book to you, if anything ever happened to her."

Hannah's eyes went wide. "Wow, that was so thoughtful of her. Especially because I only met her once, and that was months ago when my mom and dad took me to her house. She had some antique furniture that she wanted to sell so she called my parents to come buy it."

Hannah took the book from me and read the cover. Then she gasped.

"What is it?" Daisy asked.

"I recognize this book!" Hannah exclaimed. "It's an old book of poetry. I think it's about a hundred years old. I saw it when I was at Aunt Melvinia's house! I told her how much I love old poetry and she showed me this book. I practically couldn't stop reading it when I was there. I never dreamed she'd want me to have it now."

Hannah looked up at us with tears in her eyes. "Thanks so much for bringing this to me. Your Aunt Melvinia was so nice to me, especially after I told her that I was your friend."

I smiled at her. "I'm glad you like it. My dad said it was Aunt Melvinia's favorite. She kept it on her nightstand."

"Then I'll keep it on my nightstand, too," Hannah said with a gleam in her blue eyes. "I can hardly wait to read it."

And she wasn't kidding. While Daisy and I shoveled lasagna into our mouths, Hannah began to thumb through the book. It was like she completely forgot about lunch. She didn't stop until she came to the back of the book.

Then her eyebrows crinkled together. "Oh, no, this is too bad. It looks like there's some damage back here."

At that exact moment, Daisy began to toy with her bracelet.

Okay, a part of me was dying to know what was going to happen next. I wondered if Daisy was going to announce some new mystery that she had suddenly figured out. I had to admit, we'd had so much fun solving her cases!

But another part of me wanted to crawl under the table. I didn't know if I could handle a mystery today, of all days. This was the day when I was supposed to pick my one item from Aunt Melvinia's house. And as far as I was concerned, it wasn't going to be easy to choose that one thing.

Daisy looked at Hannah. "Could I please see that book?"

"Sure," Hannah said and passed it to her.

Daisy looked at the front cover and then at the back cover. She let her fingernails slide over the rough cloth on the outside of the book. Then she examined the back pages. Finally, she put it up to her nose and sniffed.

Hopefully, she wasn't searching for the scent of geraniums again.

"Hmmm . . ." she said after what seemed like the longest time. "It looks like the damage to these back pages is new. Water probably. I'd guess your Aunt Melvinia had it open on her nightstand and then spilled a glass of water on it."

I glanced over at the book. "It looks like you can still read the poetry okay. But the pages are just a little crumpled."

Daisy continued to examine it. "Hmmm . . . Something just isn't right here." She started to turn one page at a time and looked at each one carefully. I sure wanted to know what she was doing. But I knew better than to interrupt her whenever she was like this.

"Wait a minute!" Daisy finally exclaimed. "Something is different here! This page doesn't have any writing it."

Now the gears in her head seemed to go into fast forward. She started to wiggle one of the pages until it came loose. Then she carefully pulled it from the book. "This isn't part of the book at all!" she said.

She held up the ivory-colored paper that had been folded in half. Then she slowly unfolded it to reveal smeared handwriting on the inside. "It's a letter! Your Aunt Melvinia must have stuck it in the book."

Hannah leaned over to take a better look. "Wow, too bad we can't read it. It looks like the ink ran when the paper got soaked with water."

Suddenly Daisy looked up and grinned at me. "Oh, I think we can read it all right. Sally, are you thinking what I'm thinking?"

You bet I was. She wanted to use the WREB to

read the letter.

"I'm one step ahead of you," I said as I pulled the WREB from my pocket. I pushed the buttons to turn it on and passed it to Daisy to let her do the honors.

Hannah giggled. "Let me guess. This must be Sally's latest invention."

Daisy nodded at her. "You've got it!" The WREB whirred for a few minutes, and then she held it over the letter.

"And let me guess again," Hannah went on. "I'll bet that little box lets you read writing that's been ruined."

"Right again. This thing is so amazing!" Daisy continued to stare at the letter. "I can read the whole thing like Aunt Melvinia had just finished writing it."

"What does it say?" Hannah practically bounced in her chair.

"It says," Daisy began slowly, "Dear Hannah, Please ask Sally to take care of my most precious possession. Please ask her to take good care of my precious Ming. Signed, Melvinia."

Hannah gasped and practically started to choke.

I handed her a glass of water. "What's wrong?"

Boy, it seemed like it took forever for her to catch her breath again. What was a Ming, anyway? Was it something bad? Obviously, it had Hannah pretty shook up.

She finally recovered. She looked at me and then at Daisy. "Do you know what a Ming is?"

The suspense was going to kill me. "No. What is it?"

"My mom and dad talk about them all the time."

She paused and took a deep breath. "A Ming is a very, very old piece of pottery. It's from the Ming Dynasty, in China. But get this! The Ming Dynasty was around almost three-hundred to six-hundred years ago. Finding a Ming is almost the most fabulous thing ever!"

For some reason, my brain just refused to take in what Hannah was saying. "Huh? What?" I heard coming from my own mouth. "How many years did you say?"

"Three-hundred to six-hundred years ago. I did a report on the Ming Dynasty for a history project last year. The Ming Dynasty went from the late 1300s and lasted until sometime in the 1600s. It was a very famous time in history."

I felt my eyes go wide. "Holy Cannoli! You're telling me that Aunt Melvinia's Ming might be six-hundred years old?"

"Uh-huh," Hannah nodded.

"Wowser! That's absolutely ancient!" I tried to think of anything that might be as old as a Ming. At the moment, I couldn't think of a thing. Sure, I always thought my grandmas and grandpas were really old, but even they weren't as old as a Ming.

"That's right," Hannah said. "A Ming is really, really old. Because they're so old, they're really rare, too. A Ming is probably worth a gazillion dollars."

Daisy jumped to her feet. "We don't have much time! Especially since all your Aunt's stuff is going to be in that auction next week!" She handed the WREB to me and put Aunt Melvinia's letter in her pocket.

"Oh, no!" I felt my heart begin to pound. "This is

the last day for me to pick my item. The house and all the stuff in it will be turned over to the auction company tomorrow!" I put the WREB in my pocket.

Daisy skipped to the dining room door. "Then we'd better hurry! Hannah, would you know a Ming if you saw one?"

Hannah nodded. "Uh-huh. I've seen lots of pictures of them. They're really pretty."

"Good!" Daisy said. "Then we'd better get over there quick and find that Ming!"

She motioned for us to follow, and we didn't waste any time flying to the front door.

I signaled to Holmes, and, as if he could read my mind, he jumped up, put his violin away, and followed us out the door. We ran to the car and hopped inside before he'd even made it halfway down the walk. We were buckled and ready to go in the backseat when he got in and started the engine.

"In a bit of a hurry, are we ladies?" he asked as he pulled away from the curb.

"Yes, Holmes, we are," I told him. "To Aunt Melvinia's house, please. And step on it."

Daisy grinned. "Looks like we've stumbled onto another mystery after all."

I rolled my eyes and smiled. "I'm not surprised."

"Me neither," Hannah giggled.

"Because everybody knows," Hannah and I said together. "That wherever Daisy Diamond goes, a mystery is sure to follow."

CHAPTER 3

"Can't we go any faster?" I asked Holmes from the backseat of the car.

Beside me, Daisy and Hannah were about to burst at the seams with excitement. Just like I was. And it seemed like it was taking absolutely forever to get to Aunt Melvinia's house. I was just sure I was going to die if I had to wait another minute to get there.

Holmes turned down the violin music on the radio. Then he glanced at us from his rearview mirror. "I'm sorry, Ms. Sally, but I won't drive over the speed limit. I'd prefer to have everyone arrive in one piece."

Daisy patted my hand. "He's right, you know. We need to get there safe and sound so we can find this

Ming."

I crinkled my eyebrows at her. It was true.
Holmes and Daisy were both right, and I knew it. But
it didn't make the waiting any easier. I felt like saying
something sarcastic, but I held my tongue instead.
After all, Daisy was only repeating something her dad
would have said. Detective Dan Diamond had been
one of the best police officers in Pinecrest. All of us
kids liked him, and so did the grown-ups.

It was a sad day for everybody when Daisy's mom
and dad went missing in the Amazon five months
ago. But Daisy has never given up hope that they will
be found. And for the time being, she lives with her
grandma, just a few blocks from my house.

That is, when she's not practically living at my
house. Sometimes my mom and dad act like they're
her parents, too. I guess that makes her my sister in
a way. I like that idea.

I looked out the window at the houses that seemed
like they were barely creeping past. But instead of
complaining, I decided to act my age. Girls like me
who had just turned thirteen were supposed to act a
little more mature.

Sometimes it wasn't easy being mature.

"I wonder where Aunt Melvinia kept her Ming,"
I said to Daisy and Hannah. "It's funny, my dad
never said anything about a Ming. It's been months
and months since I've been to her house, but I don't
remember ever seeing any old pottery."

"Hmmm . . . That's odd," Daisy said. "But
hopefully we can find it without too much trouble."

I felt my heart begin to pound. "Oh, no! Do you

think something could've happened to it already?"

Okay, so maybe I wasn't really up for acting mature at the moment.

"We won't know till we get there," Daisy said. "But I think there are a couple of possibilities. Since everything gets turned over to the auction company tomorrow, I'll bet the auction company people will be there today."

"That's right," Hannah added. "They'll start making a list of all the things in the house. They'll be all over the place!"

"Maybe they can tell us where the Ming is," I suggested.

"Maybe. Or maybe not," Daisy said. "Since it was Aunt Melvinia's most precious possession, she might have hidden it somewhere."

Holy Cannoli! Now my heart started to pound like a bass drum. "Then how will we find it?"

Hannah smiled and nodded at Daisy. "Daisy will find it. Remember when she found the prize poodle that somebody stole from the Pinecrest dog show? Remember how Mrs. Pekinpaw cried when she got her dog back?"

"I know. I remember it well. That's the mystery where I got home late and my mom grounded me." I made a funny face at Daisy.

She grinned back at me.

"Daisy won't let you down. She always solves the case," Hannah reminded me.

I took a deep breath. It was true. Daisy always did solve the case. I was so glad I had my friends with me. If they say two heads are better than one, then I guess three heads are best of all.

And if nothing else, at least I'd made my decision about which item to choose from Aunt Melvinia's house. Of course, I planned to take the Ming. If it was Aunt Melvinia's most precious possession, then I would take care of it for her. Just like she wanted. Just like I would want someone to take care of my precious inventions if something ever happened to me.

It was funny, but for the first time, I realized that Aunt Melvinia and I had something in common. I suddenly wondered what she had been like when she was my age.

But by the time we finally arrived at Aunt Melvinia's house, I was sure my age had gone up a few years.

Her house looked exactly like I remembered it. Actually, the place looks more like a castle than a house. It was mostly built out of beige-colored stones, and it was probably as old as Hannah's house. There were big, wide stone steps that led to the front porch, which had two enormous round white columns. Flower gardens went all around the house, and they were filled with pink, red, purple and yellow flowers.

"Wow," Hannah said when Holmes parked the car in front. "This place is even prettier than I remembered. It's such a wonderful house!"

"It's beautiful," Daisy agreed. "But it's also huge. That means there could be lots of hiding places."

A dirty white van was already parked in the driveway. The words "Snodgrass Auctions" were printed in big black letters on the side of the van.

Holmes stepped out of the car and held the rear door open for us. He bowed as we jumped out of the car. "Your father said you may go on inside, Ms. Sally. It is not necessary for you to knock. The man in charge of the auction will be looking around and taking inventory today. Please let him know who you are and that you're choosing an item to take home with you. I will be right here if you should need me."

"Thank-you, Holmes," I said before all of us girls went racing up the stone steps.

We reached the front door and I opened it without knocking, just like Holmes had told me to do. Then we all ran into the front hall.

Like I'd said, I hadn't been inside Aunt Melvinia's house in months and months. But when I walked in the front door, it looked just like it did the last time I was here. The front part reminded me of a jungle. Potted plants were everywhere. Some of them had grown as tall as the two-story high ceiling. If it took a green thumb to grow plants, then Aunt Melvinia must have had the greenest thumb of all.

The plants had almost grown over all the paintings with gold-frames on the front wall. Some of those paintings were strange pictures of men with long hair and swords. Others looked a little like pictures I've seen of George Washington. Same clothes, different faces. Then there was a painting of a very handsome man standing in front of an airplane with two wings. One of the wings was just a few feet above the other wing. What a cool looking plane!

A painting of a young girl caught my eye. Funny, I'd never noticed it before. She had beautiful golden-brown curls and a red ribbon tied in her hair. In the picture, she looked like she was probably the same age as I was, but her clothes were really old-fashioned. She was the only one smiling in any of the paintings. If you put some jeans and tennis shoes on her, she would have fit in with the rest of us. I wondered who she was.

Could she have been Aunt Melvinia, when she was just a kid? I'd have to remember to ask my Dad if he knew.

I noticed that all the pictures had gold frames. In fact, gold-colored stuff was everywhere. Small gold statues, gold lamps, and gold pots for the plants. I guess Aunt Melvinia really liked gold things.

I motioned for Daisy and Hannah to follow me. We had just started to walk past the entryway when someone yelled at us.

"Halt! Stop right there! Don't take another step!" hollered a very skinny man in a black suit. "Who gave you permission to enter this building?"

The man had a long, pointy nose and thin little glasses. His beady eyes were almost as dark as his suit, and when he spoke, it sounded like he was talking directly through his nose. He didn't exactly seem like the friendly type.

I stepped forward to identify myself. "My name is Sally Sosmart and these are my friends, Daisy Diamond and Hannah Hystory. My dad said . . ."

But the beady-eyed guy didn't even let me finish. He interrupted me before I could say anything else. Didn't he know that was rude?

"Oh, yes," he said. "That's right. Your father said

you would be coming. My name is Sloan Snodgrass and I am in charge of the auction. I've got a lot of work to do, as you can see. So please pick whatever item you would like and then get out of here. I don't need you girls in my hair all day."

Well, to tell you the truth, I didn't exactly want him in my hair either. The sooner I got my Ming and got out, the better, as far as I was concerned.

"I will take the Ming," I told him.

His beady eyes got as big as tennis balls behind his skinny little glasses. He thunked his hand to his chest. "The . . . what?"

Obviously the guy had a lot to learn about listening to people. "The Ming, please," I repeated.

"There's a Ming in the house?" Mr. Snodgrass started to choke. "Why didn't anyone tell me there was a Ming in this house?"

I suddenly felt disappointed. "You mean, you haven't seen it?"

"Good heavens, young lady, of course I haven't seen it! I would give my eyeteeth to get my hands on something of that value. I've been waiting my whole life to add a Ming to my collection. Now you're telling me there's one in this house?"

Suddenly Daisy jumped in front of me. "Oh, did my friend say Ming?" She laughed a loud, kind of ho-ho-ho laugh. "Oh, no, she didn't mean Ming. She meant 'ring.' That's right. Ring. You'll have to excuse my friend. Sometimes she gets her Ms and her Rs mixed up. She wanted to see her Aunt's ring."

"Huh?" I said.

I wondered why Daisy was standing right in front

of me. I tried to step to her right, but she stepped in front of me again. So then I stepped left, and she stepped right smack in front of me once more. What in the world was she doing?

"Excuse me," I said. "But I would like to see . . ."

This time it was Hannah who interrupted me. But not by speaking. Oh, no. She interrupted me by putting her hand directly over my mouth so I couldn't say a word.

Had everyone around me suddenly lost their manners?

Hannah also laughed in a very strange way. Not ho-ho-ho like Daisy did, but more of a tee-hee-hee kind of laugh. Then she said, "like Daisy said, you'll have to excuse our friend. She would like to see some rings."

Mr. Snodgrass glared at Daisy through squinted eyes. "You mean there is no Ming?"

Daisy gave him her brightest smile. "None that we've ever seen."

Mr. Snodgrass looked from Daisy to Hannah to me, with my mouth covered by Hannah's hand, and then back again. He clenched his teeth and a vein popped out on his forehead. "You'll find her Aunt's rings upstairs in the bedroom. Be sure that you only take one. Don't steal anything."

Without letting me say a word, Daisy and Hannah practically dragged me away.

Daisy said under her breath, "Don't steal anything, yourself." Obviously, she meant Mr. Snodgrass.

My friends pulled me past the dining room and

the parlor, until we reached the huge curved staircase. Then Hannah finally removed her hand.

Okay, it was time for my friends to explain themselves. "Why did you do that?" I demanded with my hands on my hips. I'd seen my mom take that pose a hundred times and it usually got results in a hurry. "So why did you two jump in and shut me up like that?"

"I don't trust that man," Daisy said. "If he wants to add a Ming to his collection, he might start searching for your Aunt's Ming himself. Then he might steal it. I think it's best not to give him too much information."

I felt my eyes go wide. "Wowser! I never thought of that! Do you think he bought your story about the ring?"

Daisy grabbed onto the smooth wood railing. "I don't know. But I think we'd better find that Ming as quick as we can."

Hannah stepped onto the bottom stair of the marble staircase. "I agree. I've met some antique collectors who will stop at nothing to get something really old and valuable. And I don't trust that man one bit."

"Me, either," Daisy agreed. "But at least he accidentally told us some important information."

"What's that?" I asked as we all started to climb the stairs.

"At least we know the Ming isn't in plain sight," Daisy said. "If it was, Sloan Snodgrass would have found it already."

"You're right," Hannah added. "I know auction

companies always look around first before they start making lists of things. Mr. Snodgrass would have seen the Ming if it was in plain sight. And I'll bet lots of other people would know about it, too."

I heard a sigh escape from my lips. "I hope we find it before Mr. Snodgrass does."

"Let's go to the bedroom so we don't look suspicious," Daisy said. "It's a good place to start looking anyway. A lot of people keep their most valuable stuff in their bedrooms."

"Follow me," I told them. "I remember where her bedroom is."

The three of us practically flew up the stairs. At the top, I turned right. Daisy and Hannah followed me, and we headed down a long hallway.

The hallway didn't have a lot of lights, so it was pretty dark. Even so, I could still see the faded wallpaper peeling off the walls. On both sides of the hallway, there were small tables covered with little gold and glass knickknacks — and dust! Everything was covered with dust.

Hannah began to sneeze and Daisy handed her a tissue from her pocket. But it didn't slow us down. We raced past closed door after closed door, all the way to the end of the hall. At last, we stopped in front of the closed, double doors to Aunt Melvinia's bedroom.

I was practically out of breath when we got there. "This is it," I told them.

Daisy began to toy with the beads on her bracelet. "Just remember," she told us, "we might not find the Ming in here. But even if we don't, we might still uncover some clues that tell us where the Ming is."

"We're going to find it," Hannah insisted. "I just know we will! Together we make such a great team!"

"Okay," Daisy said. "Then let's do it. Go team!"

"Go team!" Hannah and I shouted back.

I opened the doors of the bedroom and we all stepped inside.

Then we all stopped dead in our tracks. My jaw practically dropped to the floor.

Our mouths all gaped wide open as we looked from one side to the other. The bedroom was enormous. And it was absolutely piled full of stuff. Newspapers, knickknacks, photographs, jewelry and so much stuff I could hardly believe it. There wasn't a single inch of the room that wasn't covered with something.

Holy Cannoli! If Daisy thought my room was messy, it was nothing compared to my Aunt Melvinia's room.

"Oh, no," Daisy cried. "This is going to take forever! And we've only got until tonight to find the Ming!"

CHAPTER 4

For a minute or two, I thought Daisy was going to fall over. I'd never seen that look on her face before, except the time when her dog really did eat her homework. Her eyes were wide and she looked kind of pale. She swayed just a little bit as she glanced from one end of Aunt Melvinia's bedroom to the other. She just kept saying over and over again, "I've never seen so much stuff in my whole life."

I guess the room must have been a real shocker for my friend who liked things to be neat and clean.

As for me, I wasn't so shook up about the place. Maybe I was just used to being around a lot of clutter. See, there really were advantages to having a messy room. I planned to remember this moment and mention it to my mom the next time she and I "discussed" keeping my room clean.

Beside me, I heard Daisy suck in a deep breath. I knew what that meant. It was her way of gathering up her courage. I'd seen her do it a thousand times. Whenever we were about to dive headlong into some scary adventure, she would take a deep breath and then jump right in. It must work for her, because she is the bravest girl I know.

She looked at me and then at Hannah. "Okay, girls," she said. "We don't have much time, so we'd better get to work. I think it would be a good idea if we each searched a different part of this bedroom."

"I agree," Hannah said as she bounced up and down.

"Me, too," I told them. After all, I trusted Daisy. When it came to investigating, she knew what she was doing.

Daisy turned to me. "Maybe it would be best if you looked through all the stuff on the dressers and in the drawers. You know, all the private stuff. Since Aunt Melvinia was your relative."

I gave her a salute. "I'm on it!"

Then she turned to Hannah. "Would you like to start searching in that huge closet over there? I think a bedroom closet is exactly where someone might keep a prize possession." Daisy pointed to the doors with sparkly crystal doorknobs at the back of the room. The doors looked different from the rest of the light-colored wood that paneled the place. Instead, the doors were made from a dark, kind of red-colored wood. Just like all the furniture in the room.

Hannah nodded. "Uh-huh! It would be a perfect place to hide a Ming. I keep some of my best stuff in my own closet!"

Daisy looked around again. "I'm going to open the curtains and get some more light in here first. Then I'll look through those framed photographs piled against the wall. Maybe I'll find a picture of the Ming. Then we can track down which room the picture was taken in, which might lead us to the Ming itself."

She pointed to the other side of the bedroom. "After that, I'll look under the bed, and after that, I'll search that old desk over there. I have a hunch we'll either find the Ming or a clue that leads us to it."

That's when she began to play with the beaded bracelet on her wrist.

And that's when my heart began to pound. I watched her twist those beads around and around, and I just knew we were going to find something.

Daisy's dark eyes sparkled. "Is everybody ready? We don't have much time!"

"We're ready!" Hannah and I yelled together.

"Then go team!" Daisy hollered.

I raced to the first dresser that was covered with things like perfume jars, old letters and cat ornaments. Hannah ran for the closet like she was running a relay race. She flung the doors open wide and jumped back just in the nick of time. Several large hatboxes came tumbling down and barely missed her.

Daisy raced to the middle of the heavy blue velvet curtains that covered the long window. She parted the curtains in the middle and pulled the right side over to the right end of the window. She tied the curtain back with a gold cord that was fastened to the wall. Then she did the same to the left side of the curtains. Once the curtains were tied back, sunlight came pouring in.

"Yay!" Hannah and I both cheered.

Now that daylight streamed in, we could see so much better! It definitely made our search easier.

I picked up an old purse from the top of the dresser. It was small and covered with tiny beads, and it had a belt loop on the back. I had never seen one like it in my life.

I held the purse up so Hannah and Daisy could see it. "Look at this! Isn't this different?"

Daisy glanced up from a stack of framed photographs that she'd been looking through. From where I stood, I could see a picture of some people waving from an ocean liner, and another picture of a girl on a swing.

"Oh, wow, that's so pretty!" Daisy exclaimed. "Be sure to check inside."

Hannah came over to see the purse. A big smile crossed her face and her blue eyes lit up like somebody had turned a flashlight on inside her. "Oh, this is so fabulous! It looks like a flapper's purse! That means it's probably from the 1920s. Lots of times the flappers kept their purses on their belts, or they tied them to their dresses. That way they kept their hands free while they were dancing. I've read lots about the flappers."

"A flapper? What's a flapper?" I'd never heard

the word before.

"That's what they called some of the ladies in the Roaring 20s," Hannah said. "Flappers wore shorter dresses that were loose at the waist. They danced the Charleston, and they got their name because they left their shoes unbuckled. So they made a flapping noise when they danced. They were so wonderful! But back then, lots of people thought flappers were just too wild and too confident."

Hannah went over to the closet and pulled out a purple dress. The dress looked like a long, loose tank top and was covered with beads. "Look," she said, "here's a flapper dress. And look at this hat! It's totally fabulous! They called it a cloche and it fit very tight on a lady's head."

Just like the purse, the hat had lots of beads on it, too. I tried to pull it over my head but my ponytail got in the way.

"What if someone had long hair?" I asked. "Wouldn't it get all messed up with a really tight hat?"

Hannah shook her head. "Oh, no! Most of the flappers bobbed their hair. People thought they were very daring!"

"Bobbed?" Daisy repeated as she continued to look through pictures.

Hannah held the dress in front of her and danced a few steps to the Charleston. "Uh-huh. It was the word they used in those days. It means they cut it short. Before that, women always had to have long hair. People thought the flappers were really wild because of it."

"Because they cut their hair?" I opened the purse and put my hand inside. The only things I found were a gold lipstick tube and a gold compact with powder in it.

Hannah put the dress back and continued her search. "I know, it's kind of hard to believe. But there was a time when people thought women should only have long hair. Can you imagine?"

I twirled the ends of my ponytail. "That's unbelievable."

"A lot of things have changed since then," Daisy added. She continued to look through the stack of framed pictures. I saw her glance at a picture of a black cat and another picture of a man standing beside an old airplane. She pulled the picture of the man out from the stack and put it to the side.

"Wowser," I sighed. "So my Aunt Melvinia must have been a flapper. She must have danced the Charleston and been really confident, and all those things. Isn't it funny? In the 1920s, she was probably a really modern woman."

"Hey! I'll bet this is her," Daisy said as she pulled another picture from the pile. "This must be a picture of Aunt Melvinia and two of her friends." She brought the picture over for Hannah and me to see.

Sure enough, one of the girls in the picture had on the same dress and hat that Hannah had found in the closet. The girl looked like a much, much, much younger Aunt Melvinia.

Holy Cannoli! I could hardly believe it. "She looks so different!" I said to my friends. The Aunt Melvinia in the picture was probably only six or seven years older than I was.

"She was really pretty," Hannah said. "She looks so happy, too."

And she did look happy. Suddenly, I wondered what Aunt Melvinia had been like back then. I wished I could go back in time and meet her. Wouldn't it be fun to wear flapper dresses and dance the Charleston?

As the three of us got back to work searching for clues, I couldn't help but think about Aunt Melvinia. What had her life been like? Had it been full of fun and interesting adventures? Did she have any sisters, or a rotten little brother like Scare'em Aaron? Were her friends a lot like my friends?

For some reason, I was more determined than ever to find her Ming and take very, very good care of it.

But so far, we hadn't had any luck at all. I looked through drawers and drawers full of her stuff, mostly clothes and things. There was no pottery hidden there, or anything that said where the Ming might be hidden. Hannah went through every inch of the closet, but didn't find anything either.

Daisy carefully looked at every framed picture in the pile, and then went through the stacks of newspapers and other junk under the bed.

But there was no Ming.

Okay, I know I was supposed to act mature and everything, but at that moment, I wasn't exactly feeling very mature. I felt a lot like a little kid who was told she couldn't go out to play. Things weren't going my way and I didn't like it one bit.

I started to wonder if we would ever find the

Ming. It felt like a thousand pounds weighed down my shoulders as I plopped onto the bed. I couldn't remember ever feeling so discouraged. Hannah fell onto the bed beside me while Daisy leaned against the wood-paneled wall.

"Don't give up yet," Daisy told us. "Maybe we'll find something when I look through all the stuff in Aunt Melvinia's desk."

I hoped she was right. I leaned back against the pillows and tried to work on my attitude a little bit. A mature person wouldn't give up easily. I couldn't let my discouragement slow me down from searching for the Ming.

Daisy closed her eyes for a moment and rubbed her forehead. With a sigh, she let her arms flop against the wall.

Then her eyes flew open wide. "Did you hear that," she said in a whisper.

"What?" I whispered back. I sat up straight. I could feel goose bumps on the back of my neck, but I didn't know why.

Hannah's eyes went wide. "I didn't hear a thing," she whispered, too. "What did you hear?"

Daisy raised her arms and let them drop against the paneled wall again. It made kind of a "thunk-thunk" noise.

Her eyebrows arched on her forehead. "That. Did you hear that?"

Okay, this was one of those moments when I felt like my friend was on another planet. Maybe she had been working too hard and needed a break.

"Sure," I told her. "I heard that."

"Me, too," Hannah agreed. "Why?"

Instead of answering, Daisy turned and faced the wall. Then she started thumping it with her fist as she moved along the paneling.

What in the world was she doing? I looked at Hannah and she looked back at me. I wondered if we should take Daisy outside for a little fresh air.

"Ah-ha!" Daisy finally hollered. She hit the wall a few more times. "Just as I thought! There is a hollow space here."

Now Hannah jumped up to join her. Had my friends completely lost their minds?

I watched in amazement as both my friends thumped their fists on the wall and walked back and forth. Now I wondered if I should go and fetch Holmes to take them both home.

Daisy moved toward one end of the wall, thumping as she went. When the thumping noise sounded different, she stopped. Then she directed Hannah to move in the opposite direction. Hannah thumped her fist along the wall just like Daisy had done. Again, when the thumping noise sounded different, she told Hannah to stop.

Then Daisy took a few steps back and stared at the wall. "I should've figured this out when we got here," she said and shook her head.

I had no idea what she thought she should have figured out. All I knew was, we had to get back to searching for that Ming or we would never find it.

Just as I was about to say something, Daisy stepped toward the wall again. She reached up and grabbed a black iron thing that jutted out from the paneling. I think my mom would have called it a wall sconce. It held one candle and made a pretty cool decoration.

But apparently my friend Daisy didn't think so. First she took the candle off the wall sconce. Then she grabbed the sconce and practically twisted it off the wall.

Before I could ask her what she was doing, I heard this weird kind of sliding, scraping noise. Then a small section of the paneling started to move.

I jumped off the bed, not sure whether I should run away or look closer. Daisy and Hannah stepped back a little. Then Hannah bounced up and down, and Daisy cheered.

The section of the wall kept sliding slowly open. One side looked like it had kind of a hinge, so the section of the wall opened up like a door. Except that nobody was opening it. It was opening up all by itself.

Pretty creepy stuff, if you ask me. I suddenly started to get goose bumps on top of my goose bumps. What was going on? Was there a ghost in this house?

Finally, after what seemed like hours, the wall stopped moving. Daisy and Hannah jumped toward the opening, and I followed behind. Inside the opening, I could barely see a brick wall and a wooden floor. The whole area was pitch black and smelled kind of damp and musty. This was one place that would give Daisy's nose a run for her money.

"What is this place?" I finally asked.

"Exactly what I was hoping for," Daisy answered with a grin. "Your Aunt Melvinia's house has a secret passageway."

I gulped and looked at the cobwebs hanging from the ceiling inside that passageway. "We're not going in there, are we?"

I heard Daisy take a deep breath and saw her toying with her bracelet. I guess I already knew the answer to that question.

We were definitely going in. Holy Cannoli!

CHAPTER 5

With one hand, Daisy swiped the cobwebs and pulled them down. "Let's see what's back here," she said as she stepped into the dark opening of the secret passageway. She disappeared into the blackness while Hannah and I stood frozen in place.

Was she kidding? She wanted *me* to go and see what was back there? Maybe she could go visit that place all by herself and just send me a nice postcard. You know, the kind that says, "Missing you. Wish you were here." Because, going into that dark opening wasn't exactly my idea of a fun time.

Thankfully, seconds later, she popped her head back out. A frown crossed her face. "It's too dark in there," she said to Hannah and me.

As if I hadn't already figured that one out.

Daisy grabbed the candle she had already removed from the wall sconce. It looked just like the candles my mom had all over our house. It was about five inches tall and kind of fat, and it smelled like some kind of flower. I had no idea why Daisy was suddenly so interested in that candle.

I also had no idea why she suddenly started to open the drawers in Aunt Melvinia's desk. She pulled one drawer open at a time and then rummaged through all the stuff inside. Then she would slam the drawer shut and pull open another one. Apparently, she was in a very big hurry.

What was going on?

At last, I heard her yell "Ah-ha!" She grabbed a package of matches from the drawer.

Before I could say a word, she swiped one of the matches against the package edge. It instantly flamed at the tip, and then she touched it to the wick of the candle.

Within seconds, the candle was lit.

That's when I finally figured out what she was doing.

I watched her blow the match out and pick up the candle. Her dark eyes beamed even brighter than the flame on top of that candle. She grinned at Hannah and me and said, "Ready to go?"

Okay, I have to admit, I wasn't ready at all! And for that matter, I didn't think I'd ever really be ready to step into that dark secret passageway. But I knew there was no use mentioning that I was pretty scared about wandering in there. Sure, I could have thrown a fit and refused to go. But what kind of a person would I be if I did that? Especially since my friends were willing to step into that dark space to help me search for Aunt Melvinia's Ming.

No, there was no way I could refuse. I had to go in there, whether I liked it or not. I decided not to be a really big baby about it.

I grabbed onto Hannah's sleeve and she grabbed onto the back of Daisy's shirt. Then the three of us shuffled our feet and moved directly into the dark opening. Sure, that candle may have been lit, but it wasn't exactly as bright as the sun shining into Aunt Melvinia's bedroom.

Or, maybe I should have said, the sun that *was* shining into Aunt Melvinia's bedroom. I took one last look behind me and noticed some dark clouds forming in the sky outside the window. It looked like a storm was heading our way.

Holy Cannoli! Just what I needed! Even though I am thirteen, I hate to admit it, but I'm not exactly crazy about thunderstorms. Well, all right, the truth be told, thunder and lightening give me the heebie-jeebies. Whenever a bad storm starts to brew, I could happily crawl into bed and pull the covers over my head.

Now I wondered if we should be entering this great dark cavern ahead of us with a storm picking up.

"Um. . . excuse me . . ." I said to the other girls. "Did you know we've got a thunderstorm heading our way?"

Daisy's muffled voice floated back to me. "Uh-huh. Should be a real bang-a-roo."

How could I forget? My friend Daisy loves a good storm. She always says it adds some excitement to the air. Obviously, even a storm outside wasn't going to stop us from going farther and farther into that dark secret passageway.

By now we had probably gone about ten feet, but it felt like a thousand to me. My shoulder scraped against the brick wall a couple of times, and I could feel dirt and dust scraping under my shoes.

Then suddenly there was this huge explosion of noise! It was probably the loudest thing I've ever heard in my life! I instantly fell to my feet and ducked for cover. Daisy and Hannah did the same.

Had we come to the end of our lives here in this dark secret passageway? Surely we weren't going to make it out of here alive! Because that noise must have come from some big, giant monster that planned to eat us for an afternoon snack. I kneeled in the darkness and started to say my prayers.

That's when I heard a second strange noise. Giggling.

Yup, that's right. Beside me, Hannah and Daisy giggled. I wondered what could be so funny when we were about to be eaten by some giant monster.

I figured out the answer to that one when I heard the first noise again. Beside me, Hannah sneezed. But inside this long, dark tunnel, it sounded like a cannon had gone off.

I started to giggle along with my friends. All of a sudden, the whole situation seemed kind of funny.

Wowser, I never thought a sneeze could sound so scary!

I stood up just as Hannah sneezed again. But this time I didn't fall to the floor. Instead, I pulled a tissue from my pocket and handed it to her.

"Thanks," she said. She stood up and blew her nose. "All this dust is killing my allergies."

"Don't worry," Daisy said. "We won't be in here long. Just long enough to see where this secret passageway goes and to search for clues. Then we'll get out of here."

Well, at least that was a relief!

I grabbed onto Hannah's arm again and started following my friends once more. Just ahead of me I could see the dim light of the candle. I hoped and prayed it wouldn't go out before we got to wherever we were going.

Up in front I heard Daisy say, "It looks like the passage branches off here. Which way would you like to go? Right or left?"

I wanted desperately to say, "back." But before I could say a word, Hannah spoke up. "Let's go to the right."

"Okay," Daisy said. "We'll go to the right."

The light of the candle grew even dimmer as Daisy turned the corner. I felt Hannah go to the right, and I followed along, hugging the wall. With my fingers, I felt the sharp corner of the brick wall and turned to the right. Behind me, the light coming from Aunt Melvinia's bedroom disappeared from view.

"Okay," Daisy said. "Put your right hands against the wall. We're going to go down some stairs now."

I counted the steps as we moved down.

One, two, three, four, five, six, seven, eight, nine,

ten, eleven, twelve.

"Look," I heard Daisy shout. "Right over there!"

I didn't know whether to run away or just wait and see what she was talking about.

"Oh, I see it," Hannah said. "Whatever it is, it really sparkles! Even in the candlelight!"

I saw the light from the candle go downward. I could barely see a shiny object on the floor.

"We'll get a better look at it when we get back," Daisy said, her voice ringing with excitement. "I'll put it in my pocket for now."

The shiny object disappeared from view. In the same instant, I felt something small and furry go scurrying over my foot and brush past my ankle.

A mouse! It had to be!

Holy Cannoli! I nearly jumped to the ceiling!

Beside me, Hannah peeped, and I saw Daisy and the candlelight jump, too. I sucked in a deep breath, well aware that a scream was about to come out next. Before a shriek came bursting from my lips, I felt someone's hand clamp around my mouth.

This time it was Daisy's hand.

"Shhhh . . ." I heard her whisper into my ear. "Look." She turned me around to see light shining through a cluster of ten small open slits in the wall. It must have been a heating vent or something.

I peered through the opening and I could see right into an entirely different room in Aunt Melvinia's house. The pink canopy bed and wood dresser told me it was another bedroom.

A girl with long, brown hair was standing with her back to us. I could hear her talking to Mr. Snodgrass.

"Don't worry," Daisy whispered in my ear. "They can't see us."

Even though I felt butterflies zooming around in my stomach, I knew my friend was right. After all, I am a scientist. And I saw right away that the people in the room were a long, long way from the vent. Plus, they were standing in the light, and we were standing in the dark. That's how I knew we were hidden from their sight. Sometimes it really pays to be a scientist!

In any case, was I ever thankful they couldn't see us! Especially since it looked like the girl and Mr. Snodgrass were having an argument.

"Now, look here," the girl said. "I don't care who you are or what you think you're supposed to be doing."

Then Mr. Snodgrass said, "Perhaps if you had phoned to let us know you were coming."

The girl with the brown hair said, "It doesn't matter. She was my Aunt . . . or something like that. Anyway, I've got every right to be here if I want to. And just like all the nieces, I'm here to get my one item."

"Fine!" Mr. Snodgrass said and stomped away.

"Yes, very fine," the girl said.

I knew that voice. I'd recognize it anywhere.

It was my snotty cousin, Jewell. And just like her name, she loved jewels. All kinds of them. And apparently she also liked the ones she was taking out of a jewelry box and putting into her purse.

That's when I realized it. She was stealing stuff from Aunt Melvinia's house!

Well, you know what they say. You can't pick
your relatives. And my cousin Jewell Jasper was
not a relative I ever would've picked. Much like
I probably never would've picked my little brother,
Scare'em Aaron.

But at least my little brother knew better than to
steal stuff that didn't belong to him.

"Look," I whispered to Daisy and Hannah. "It's
my cousin. She's stealing that jewelry."

"Let's just hope she doesn't find the Ming," Daisy
whispered back to us.

That's when I felt my heart begin to pound really
loud. If Jewell knew there was something as valuable
as a Ming in the house, she would probably steal it,
too. And I just knew she wouldn't take care of it like
Aunt Melvinia had wanted.

"I've got an idea," Daisy whispered once more.
"Let's go back."

Nobody had to tell me twice that it was time to
get out of there! I turned around and accidentally
stepped on Hannah's foot in the darkness.

"Ouch!" she hollered.

This time it was my turn to cover her mouth with
my hand. The three of us froze in our tracks. From
the dark secret passageway, we all stared through the
slits in the vent. In the bedroom on the other side,
Jewell dropped another necklace into her purse and
spun around. She squinted her eyes and stared in our
direction.

It was weird standing there, with the three of us
staring at her in the room and her staring back. I
knew she couldn't see us, but now I wondered, had

she heard us?

Inside the bedroom, she took a few steps in our direction. All the while, she kept staring at the vent.

Now I wondered if she could hear the pounding of my heart, because it sure sounded plenty loud to me.

At long last, she turned and went back to looking through the jewelry box.

I felt Daisy tug on my arm and I grabbed Hannah, and the three of us vamoosed! We climbed all twelve of those steps and then took a left in the passageway. Before long, I could see the light from Aunt Melvinia's bedroom.

We had barely stepped inside the room, when Hannah started talking. "Can you believe that girl? She's taking all that stuff that doesn't belong to her! We've got to find that Ming first or she'll take it, too. We've got to stop her!"

So far my heart hadn't slowed down one bit. I looked at Hannah and then at Daisy. "I know, I know. But how?"

Daisy blew out the candle and brushed the dust from her sleeve. Then she turned the wall sconce right side up again and put the candle back into place. The door to the secret passageway closed shut, but this time, it moved a little faster than it did when we opened it.

"I've got an idea," Daisy said. "And it just might work."

Holy Cannoli! What was she up to now?

CHAPTER 6

"Hannah, please get me that flapper dress," Daisy said as we stood in Aunt Melvinia's bedroom. "And the hat, too, please. Hurry!"

"Coming right up," Hannah said. She rushed to the closet and flung the doors open wide.

Then Daisy turned to me. "Sally, please get me that flapper purse!"

I knew just what she was talking about. She wanted the little beaded purse that I'd found on Aunt Melvinia's dresser earlier. I raced over to the dresser and glanced through all the clutter until I spotted the little purse. Then I grabbed it and zoomed back to where Daisy was standing by the bed.

"Thanks," she said. "Please put it on the bed for

now."

I did just as she wanted. Normally I didn't like it when people told me what to do. Except for grown-ups, like my teacher, or maybe my mom. And if anyone else ever started bossing me around, I usually just dug in my heels and said, "no way."

But with Daisy it was different. Whenever Daisy started to bark out orders like this, I never complained a bit. Neither did Hannah. That's because we both knew Daisy well enough to know that she was hot on the trail of something big. And that something big was going to help us find the Ming.

I only wished I knew what she was up to.

When Hannah returned with the purple flapper dress, I really had to wonder. Daisy took it and immediately slid it over her head. She pulled the dress down until it fit over her t-shirt and jeans. It was a little big on her, but not too bad.

Holy Cannoli! She sure picked a strange time to play dress up! What was she going to do next, start dancing the Charleston?

Hannah and I watched in amazement as Daisy gathered her long, dark curly hair into a ponytail. Then she twisted it into a knot on top of her head. She put the flapper hat over her head, hair and all, and pulled the hat down to her ears. Wowser! That hat sure fit snug as a bug on her head!

Next, she leaned down and pulled off her tennis shoes and socks. "Sally, please tell me some stuff about your cousin. Quick!"

"There's not much to tell." I glanced for a second at the dark clouds forming in the sky outside the window. "My cousin Jewell Jasper is probably the most selfish girl I've ever met. She never thinks about anybody but herself."

"Good," Daisy said. "Then this is going to be easy."

Huh? What was going to be easy? Once again I wondered if my friend was on another planet. Because I had no idea what she was talking about, or what she had up her sleeve.

Speaking of sleeves, Daisy now rolled her t-shirt sleeves up and tucked them nicely under the top of the dress.

Then she turned to look in the mirror on Aunt Melvinia's dresser. "Does your cousin have any hobbies? Is she involved in anything at school?"

Suddenly the wind gusted outside and the branches from a tall tree scraped against the window. I nearly jumped a mile.

"She loves jewels," I said through chattering teeth. "It seems like the more she gets, the more she wants. And I think she's on the decorating committee for the Summer Festival at her school."

"Perfect," Daisy said with a grin.

I was glad *she* thought so.

She picked up the flapper purse and opened it. Then she pulled out the lipstick. She removed the lid and twisted the lipstick up into place. With a couple of swipes, she covered her lips with the bright red color.

"Omigosh, Daisy, you look so grown-up!" Hannah exclaimed. "You don't look like a kid at all! That flapper dress looks just beautiful on you."

I had to admit, my friend had aged before my very eyes. She really did look old, almost like she was thirty or something. The only thing that ruined the look was her jeans sticking out from under the dress.

As though she read my mind, she leaned down and rolled up the bottoms of her jeans. In a matter of seconds, she had them hidden neatly beneath the purple flapper dress.

"There!" she finally said. "Now I'd better go!"

"Go?" I felt my eyebrows crinkle together. "Where are you going? Would you mind filling us in?"

"No time," came Daisy's answer. "But you can come along and watch if you like."

She grabbed our hands and pulled us to the door. "Come on! We have to hurry."

The next thing I knew, I was racing to keep up with Daisy and Hannah. We practically flew out of Aunt Melvinia's room and down the hall. We ran down the marble staircase, and then Daisy suddenly stopped dead in her tracks.

Hannah and I stopped right behind her. That's when I felt my heart start to pound really hard. Wowser! What in the world was going on? Had Daisy heard Sloan Snodgrass or something?

But Daisy didn't seem to be a bit nervous. And neither did Hannah. Instead, Daisy just started to turn in a slow circle and point to all the different hallways. And believe me, there were a lot of hallways! There were hallways that went behind both sides of the stairs, and there was a hallway to the right of the stairs and to the left of the stairs. And then there was the hallway that led back to the front entryway.

Like I said, there were a lot of hallways!

Daisy pointed to each one as she took slow steps and turned two complete circles. She started to mumble to herself, too. I heard her say something about east and west, and taking the stairs, and something else. For a minute there, she seemed to be doing some kind of math problem aloud. But part of it must have been in her head, because I couldn't figure out what she was talking about.

Just as I was really starting to get worried about her, she said, "This way."

And we were off. We zoomed down the hallway that went to the right of the stairs. As soon as we got close to the first open door, Daisy slowed down. Naturally, Hannah and I slowed down with her.

Daisy put her finger to her lips to let us know we should be quiet. Then she carefully peeked into the room.

"Not here," she said in a very soft voice. "Let's keep moving."

So we followed Daisy down the hall again. The weird thing was, it wasn't like we were following Daisy at all. It was like we were following some grown-up that we'd never met before. She looked so different in her flapper getup. And I was still dying to know why she was wearing Aunt Melvinia's old clothes in the first place.

But I knew better than to ask now. I'd just have to wait until Daisy clued me in on the whole story.

When we got to the next door, Daisy carefully peeked inside again. But this time she jumped back and put her back flat against the wall.

Hannah and I also put our backs flat against the wall.

Why? I had no idea. But if Daisy did it, and we were following Daisy, it seemed like the right thing to do.

"This is it," Daisy whispered. She pointed to an open doorway across the hall. "You two stay in that room over there and keep quiet."

And that was the last thing she said before she strolled into the room beside us like she owned it. Hannah and I immediately ducked into the room on the other side of the hall where Daisy had told us to wait. The room was dark and, luckily, no one was in there. When my eyes got used to the darkness, I could see tons of stuff overflowing from bookshelves against the walls. There was a really big desk right across from us, so I figured the room must have been a study or something.

But Hannah and I didn't take time to explore. Instead, we put our backs against the wall, just like we did in the hallway. I glanced at Hannah and she smiled back at me. Hannah didn't seem a bit surprised or shook up by the whole situation.

The truth be told, I guess I shouldn't have been surprised either. After all, I'd been with Daisy on enough of her cases that nothing she did should surprise me by now.

But I nearly jumped when I heard Daisy's voice coming from the room across the hall. "Pardon me," she said in a Southern drawl, "but aren't you the famous Jewell Jasper?"

Huh? So that was the room Daisy led us to! The
room where my self-centered cousin Jewell had been
stealing jewelry!

"Oh, my, oh, my," Daisy went on. "I simply must
count my lucky stars that I ran into you here! Why,
when that nice Mr. Snodgrass told me you were here, I
was so excited I could hardly stand it!"

What in the world was Daisy up to? And when
had she suddenly developed a Southern accent?

Now it was my cousin's voice that I heard. "Yes,
I'm Jewell Jasper. And who are you?"

"Why, sugar!" Daisy went on. "Don't you
recognize me? I'm Mrs. Sue May Ellen Smith. I'm the
Assistant Librarian at your school."

"Oh, yeah? Then how come I've never seen you
before?"

"Because I only started working at your school last
week. And now the regular librarian . . . oh, my
heaven's . . . I simply can't remember her name at
the moment . . ."

"You mean, Mrs. Filbert?"

"Yes," Daisy exclaimed in her new accent. "Yes,
that's right, dear Mrs. Filbert! Such a darling! I've
never met anyone nicer!"

"Are you sure you're talking about Mrs. Filbert?
Everyone thinks she's a nasty old hag."

I could just picture my cousin Jewell as she spoke.
First she would flip her long brown hair behind her
shoulders. And then she would stand with her arms
folded across her chest, just like she always did.

"Well, now, sugar," Daisy said. "You know what
they say — If you can't say something nice about

someone, then don't say anything at all."

"Fine," Jewell said in a nasty tone. "So, what's with that outfit? I've never seen anyone wear a getup like yours!"

Now I felt my heart pound even harder inside my chest. Was Jewel about to figure out that Daisy, or rather, Mrs. Sue May Ellen Smith, wasn't a grown-up at all? What would my snotty cousin do if she realized the person she was talking to was just a girl who was even younger than she was?

Daisy's voice echoed strong and clear from across the hallway. "Why, sugar! Where I come from, clothes like this are simply all the rage! Any woman with half a fashion sense wears clothes like mine."

"Okay, fine," Jewell said. "But you still haven't told me what you want! And I'm very busy here!"

"Well, sugar, as I was about to say, Mrs. Filbert has put me in charge of the school newspaper."

"So?"

"So, of course I plan to do an article about you. After all, I hear you're on the decorating committee for the Summer Festival. But I'm really interested in your jewel collection. I understand you have absolutely exquisite taste!"

"Well, um . . . yes, I do," Jewell stammered.

"Oh, wonderful, sugar! Then I'll need a photograph of you and all your marvelous jewels! Plus I'll need to do a complete interview. Can you meet me at the school in an hour?"

"Well . . . okay."

"And please, if you don't mind, would you put on some nicer clothes? After all, you can't have your picture taken in that outfit you've got on. Not when you're wearing such exquisite jewelry."

"All right . . ."

"Oh, and please be sure to bring any new jewelry that you've collected. After all, I want my article and pictures to have only the latest information!"

"Well, okay," Jewell said. "I've got a few new pieces that I could bring. In fact, you might even say I picked them up today."

"Oh, perfect, perfect!" Daisy exclaimed. "Now, hurry along, sugar! This article could make you the most popular girl in school. You simply must look your absolute best!"

"Oh, yes, you're right! I've got just the dress I can wear."

"That's marvelous, sugar. I'll meet you in the Library in an hour. But you'd better run. You really should fix your hair a little, too."

"Oh, you're right. I'll see you in an hour!" Jewell practically shouted.

The next thing I knew, I heard her running out of the room and down the hallway. I guessed she would be outside in a matter of minutes.

Suddenly Hannah and I burst out laughing. Now I understood what Daisy had been up to! She'd been planning to get rid of Jewell since the moment we saw her from the secret passageway!

Hannah and I held our stomachs from laughing so hard. We were still laughing when we joined Daisy in the hallway.

Daisy had a huge grin on her face. "That should keep your cousin busy for a while."

I couldn't resist teasing her. "Well, Mrs. Sue May Ellen Smith. You make a pretty funny Assistant Librarian. And a really funny actress."

Daisy bowed. "Hold your applause, please. I'd better get these clothes back to Aunt Melvinia's room. And we'd better get back to work."

"You're right," Hannah said. "We still haven't found that Ming and who knows where it could be in this big house. We don't even have any clues yet."

"Don't be so sure," Daisy said.

Huh? I'd been with Daisy the whole time, and I didn't remember finding any clues. I crinkled my brows at her. "What do you mean?"

"Yeah, Daisy, what are you talking about?" Hannah chimed in. "I didn't see any clues."

Just then I noticed Daisy toying with her beaded bracelet. "I'm talking about the shiny object we found in the secret passageway," she said.

Wowser! I'd forgotten all about that!

Daisy pulled the flapper dress up over her rolled up jeans and reached into her pocket.

Suddenly my heart started to pound again. I was dying to see what she had found in that dark passageway.

She struggled for a few seconds and then pulled the item from her pocket. In the light of the hallway, I could see the object was really, *really* shiny. Sparkly, you might even say.

Holy Cannoli! That's because the whole thing looked like it was made out of diamonds.

Daisy held the object up so we could all take a better look. That's when it really hit me. The shiny object we found in the secret passageway was some kind of bracelet. And it was made from diamonds. Rows of them.

And dangling from the middle of it was the letter "M", made from gold.

CHAPTER 7

"Holy Cannoli!" My eyes felt like they were going to pop out of my head while I stared at the bracelet that Daisy was holding.

Beside me, Hannah was breathing very fast and very hard, like she had been running or something. "It must be Aunt Melvinia's bracelet," she said. "It's so beautiful. And those sure don't look like rhinestones. I've seen lots and lots of rhinestone jewelry at my mom and dad's store, and well . . . I think those stones are . . . are . . ."

"Diamonds," Daisy said calmly, as though she'd seen diamonds every day of her life. "But that just doesn't make sense."

"Huh?" I took my eyes off the bracelet for a

second and looked at her. "What doesn't make sense?"

"Well," Daisy said, "why would your Aunt Melvinia's bracelet be in the secret passageway?"

The answer to that question seemed pretty easy to me. "Maybe she lost it there. Maybe it fell off her wrist and she didn't even know it."

"Hmmm . . ." Daisy shook her head. "I'm not so sure. After all, it's a really expensive bracelet. Most people would search pretty hard if they lost something that valuable."

"Maybe she was hiding it there," Hannah suggested.

"I don't think so," Daisy said. "We found it on the floor. If Aunt Melvinia wanted to hide it, she would've put it in a crack between the bricks. Or she would've put it in a hole in the wall or some place like that."

I had to agree with that one. Besides, wouldn't the bracelet get dirty if it was hidden in there? And this bracelet barely had any dust on it, let alone a cobweb.

I shivered again as I thought about walking into that dark passageway. "I know if it was my bracelet, I'd never even wear it into that spooky old place."

"Exactly." Daisy suddenly stood up very straight. "That's why this whole thing just doesn't add up."

To be honest, I really didn't see what difference it made how the bracelet got into the secret passage anyway. Sometimes it seemed like my friend Daisy paid way too much attention to little details. Especially since it didn't have anything to do with finding the Ming. And the minutes were quickly ticking away.

I leaned in to look closer at the diamond bracelet. "What are we going to do with it?" For some reason, I was scared to touch it, like it might be really hot and burn me.

"Let's hang onto it for a little while," Daisy said. "I have a hunch it might be a very important clue." She stuffed it back into the pocket of her jeans.

Then, as though she'd read my mind about time ticking by, she said, "We'd better get back to Aunt Melvinia's bedroom. I've got to get out of these clothes."

"And we'd better get back to our search," Hannah added. "Or we'll never find that Ming!"

"Let's zoom!" I said. This time I was the one who led the way as we all raced back upstairs.

We barely stepped into Aunt Melvinia's bedroom when a streak of lightening flashed across the darkened sky. Seconds later, a huge boom of thunder echoed all around.

Wowser! I nearly jumped to the top of the tall ceiling, and Hannah almost came with me.

But as always, Daisy wasn't even startled. She pulled off the flapper hat and unknotted her hair.

I glanced at the covers on Aunt Melvinia's bed. Would Daisy and Hannah think I was a big baby if I jumped under those covers? Probably. I resisted the temptation, but believe me, it took a lot of resisting! Especially when I noticed my knees were knocking.

I turned around so my back was to the window. I figured it might not be so scary if I couldn't see the dark sky and the lightening outside.

Daisy pulled off the flapper dress and Hannah immediately hung it back in the closet. Then Daisy unrolled the sleeves of her t-shirt and the bottoms of her jeans.

"Now, I need to find a phone," she said and glanced around the room. "Surely Aunt Melvinia had a phone in here."

That was my guess, too. But with all the clutter in the room, it wasn't easy to spot a phone right away. Hannah looked on the dresser, Daisy looked on the desk and I went for the nightstands.

There wasn't a phone on the first nightstand, so I ran around the bed to the nightstand on the other side. After I removed a few magazines, there it was — a pink phone with rhinestones on it!

"I've got it!" I hollered to Daisy.

She immediately ran over and picked up the receiver. "Thanks, Sally!"

Once again, I had to wonder what she was up to. Wasn't this an odd time to be making a phone call?

"Let's just hope this phone works," she said and pushed the "Talk" button on the receiver. She held the phone to her ear, obviously checking to see if there was a dial tone.

But suddenly her dark eyes went very, very wide. She looked at both Hannah and me and held her finger to her mouth, letting us know we should be quiet.

Now what was going on? Someday I planned to invent a mind-reading machine, so I could figure out what was happening inside her head.

She held the receiver out, and I could hear someone was already talking on the line. So why didn't Daisy do the polite thing and just hang up, instead of listening in on someone else's conversation?

But the second I recognized the voice on the line, I knew why she wanted to eavesdrop. Holy Cannoli! It was Sloan Snodgrass! I didn't know who he was talking to, but I didn't like what he was saying.

Nope, I didn't like it one bit.

"Those kids let it slip," I heard him say.

"What do you mean?" asked the man he was talking to.

"They mentioned something about a Ming," Sloan said.

I clamped a hand over my mouth, to hold back the yelp that wanted to come out.

"Are you sure?" asked the other man. "Nobody said nothing about a Ming."

"Yes, I know, but I'm guessing it must have been some kind of family secret. Something that only a select few knew about."

"Yeah, but they're just a bunch of dumb kids. Why would they know anything? All they would know about is their dolls and stuff. They wouldn't know nothing about a Ming."

That comment really made me mad. Not only was that man talking about the Ming, but he was insulting us on top of everything. Who did he think he was, calling us a bunch of dumb kids? He didn't exactly sound all that smart to me.

"Oh, no," Sloan Snodgrass argued. "They weren't so dumb. In fact, these kids were a bunch of brainiacs. Together, they might figure out where the Ming is hidden."

Okay, even though I didn't like Sloan Snodgrass much, at least he was giving us a little credit. That was better than his friend. But even so, I still didn't like the whole conversation.

"Yeah, all right, Sloan, suppose you've got them figured out. Do you think they found the Ming already?"

"I don't think so, because they've been here awhile, and they're still looking around."

"Keep your eye on them. Don't let them leave the house with that Ming. Get it away from them, no matter what you have to do."

"I will take care of things, Eddie."

"I mean it, Sloan. I mean, get that Ming away from them, no matter what you have to do!"

"I shall, Eddie!"

"If you need any help taking care of those kids, I'll be there."

"I'll let you know if I need you."

"Good. Because this could be the break we've been looking for."

And that was all they said. Both men hung up, and suddenly the room seemed kind of eerie and quiet. Except for the thunder booming outside.

I stood frozen to the spot. Goose bumps jumped up all over my skin, making me shiver. What exactly did he mean, "no matter what you have to do?" Did he plan to hurt us?

Hannah's mouth was open wide and her eyes were huge. But Daisy's dark eyes looked like they had sparks coming from them. Wowser, I hardly ever saw her mad, but when she was, look out!

A dial tone came buzzing out of the receiver now and Daisy immediately started to push some buttons. She put the phone to her ear again and I heard her say, "Hi, Detective McCoy, this is Daisy Diamond calling."

I breathed a huge sigh of relief and fell backwards on to Aunt Melvinia's bed. After all, I knew who Detective McCoy was. Detective Tom McCoy was her dad's best friend, another detective with the Pinecrest Police Department.

That meant we were going to be safe. Sloan Snodgrass and his friend would never be able to hurt us. Because Daisy had called the police to report them.

"Detective Tom," I heard her say. "You might want to show up at the Pinecrest School in about an hour."

Huh? Why was she sending him to the school when she should be sending him straight to Aunt Melvinia's house? How was Detective Tom going to protect us if he went to the school?

Now Daisy said, "A girl named Jewel Jasper will be waiting there. I think you'll find she has some stolen jewelry with her."

A few seconds later, she thanked him and hung up the phone. Now I felt my mouth fall open wide. Sure, I wanted the police to get the jewelry that my cousin had stolen. But what happened to the police protection I thought Daisy was going to get for us?

I jumped up off the bed. "Daisy, why didn't you

tell the policeman to come over here? You heard what Sloan Snodgrass and his friend said!"

"Because," Daisy said, "we aren't in any real danger yet. Sloan's friend, Eddie, said to get the Ming away from us no matter what he had to do."

I started to choke. "I know. And that didn't exactly sound good to me."

"Me, either," Hannah squeaked. "Those two men sound like really nasty guys."

Daisy glanced out the window. "I'm sure they are. But Eddie isn't even here. And remember, they want the Ming as much as we do. As long as we haven't found it yet, Sloan won't touch us."

Daisy walked over to Aunt Melvinia's desk. She picked up the candle that she'd used earlier to lead us through the secret passageway.

Another flash of lightening lit up the dark sky outside and my teeth instantly started to chatter. "So what happens when we find the Ming? Sloan Snodgrass and his friend might try to hurt us if we don't give them the Ming."

Daisy grinned and pulled open one of the drawers of Aunt Melvinia's desk. "I have a plan."

Before I could argue more, a giant flash of lightening streaked across the sky. Thunder boomed just a few seconds later, and then the lights went out.

That was all I could take.

I pulled down the covers of Aunt Melvinia's bed and jumped in. Then I tugged the covers back up over my head. I snuggled down deep, where no lightening, let alone any bad guys, could ever find me.

I closed my eyes tight and tried to think happy

thoughts. I tried to imagine being at home in my laboratory, and making lots of new inventions.

It almost worked, too. For a few seconds, I completely forgot about all the bad stuff I was hiding from. That was, until I heard noises and footsteps outside my lovely little nest. That's when it dawned on me that I'd left my friends behind to face the cold, cruel world. A world of thunder and lightening, and Sloan Snodgrass. Holy Cannoli!

Well, I may a real scaredy-cat, but I'd never leave my friends behind. Not on purpose anyway. I crawled up toward the pillows at the top of the bed and peeked out.

There I saw Daisy and Hannah standing next to the bed. Daisy was holding a lighted candle in her hand.

"Are you all right?" Hannah asked. "I didn't know what happened to you. You had me scared to death. As soon as Daisy lit the candle, I couldn't find you anywhere. I thought maybe Sloan Snodgrass had grabbed you."

Daisy grinned at me. "From the sounds I heard when the lights went out, I had a good idea where you went. Especially after I noticed a big lump in Aunt Melvinia's bed."

Right at that moment, I was really glad the room was still dark, except for the light from the candle. That way nobody could see how embarrassed I was. How could I explain to them that I'd jumped under the covers because I was scared?

I had to think of something, and quick.

"Uhm. . . I was just under here looking for clues,"

I said in the most cheerful voice I could come up with. "You know, a lot of people hide things in their bed. Things like . . ." I reached my hand under the pillows and felt around. If only I could find something there.

Well, it must have been my lucky day, because I did find something. An envelope.

I pulled it out and noticed that Daisy was playing with her beaded bracelet.

Was it possible that I really did find a clue?

Hannah bounced up and down. "What is it? Hurry, let's take a look."

Daisy held the candle closer to the envelope. The paper was kind of dingy and the edges looked a little worn. I looked at it more carefully and saw it was a letter that someone had sent to Aunt Melvinia. The date was November 24, 1944.

Wowser, that was some old letter!

I started to pull the letter out of the envelope but then I stopped. After all, I was about to read someone's private mail. I don't think I'd be too happy if someone read my private letters. Especially if that someone was my little brother, Scare'em Aaron.

"Go ahead," Daisy said, as though she could read my thoughts. "I don't think Aunt Melvinia would mind. She would want us to find the Ming."

"Yeah, go ahead," Hannah agreed. "She must have kept that letter there for a reason. We should see what it says."

I took a deep breath and slowly pulled the folded-up letter from the envelope. A couple of little black and white pictures fell out.

One was a picture of three men sitting at a dinner

table. The men were all wearing soldiers' uniforms. The other was a picture of a man in a uniform standing beside an old airplane.

I recognized the man right away. He was the same man in the picture in Aunt Melvinia's front entryway. But in that picture, he was standing beside a different plane.

"C'mon," Hannah said. "Read the letter!"

I opened it up carefully and read aloud. "My dearest Melvinia, I just wanted to show you a few photographs of what things look like over here in the Pacific. The first is a picture of my buddies at dinnertime. The food's okay, but not that great. How I miss your wonderful cooking! I can hardly wait to taste your apple pie again when I get home.

"The second picture is of me standing by my P-51 Mustang. What a beautiful bird she is."

"A bird?" Hannah picked up the picture of the man. "He must mean his airplane."

Without commenting, I read on, "The fighting continues over here. It's very fierce, and a lot of good men have been killed. I hope we can take Iwo Jima. We need to take that island so we can land our planes there.

"I miss you so much, my darling, and I hope I'll be home for Christmas this year. But just in case I don't make it, I already sent you a special gift. After you unwrap it, you'll see it's in a wooden box with Chinese writing on it. I don't read Chinese so I can't tell you what it says but it's very pretty. You'll find your present inside.

"I can hardly wait to see you again! This war has

taken such a toll on all of us. As ever, your loving husband, Archie."

Hannah sighed. "Wow, that was during World War II. Archie must have been a pilot."

Daisy had tears in her eyes. "I wonder what happened to him."

I carefully folded up the letter. Then I put it and the pictures back in the envelope. "Me, too. I wonder if he made it home for Christmas."

It was funny, but I guess I never knew that Aunt Melvinia had a husband. And he was such a handsome man, too. Somehow, before today, I guess I'd never really thought much about Aunt Melvinia's life at all.

Daisy wiped her tears away with the back of her hand. It suddenly dawned on me that she was probably thinking of her own mom and dad, lost in the Amazon. She was probably wondering if they would ever come home, too.

For the first time, I realized how brave my friend Daisy was. Aunt Melvinia must have been very brave, too, waiting for Archie to come home.

"The box," Daisy said. "With the Chinese writing on it!" She turned to Hannah. "Didn't you say the Ming was Chinese?"

"Yes," Hannah barely whispered.

"Holy Cannoli!" I jumped out of the bed. "Aunt Melvinia's husband must have sent her the Ming!"

"And it's probably still in the box he sent it in," Daisy said. "If we find the box, we'll probably find the Ming."

CHAPTER 8

I don't know why, but from that moment on, I felt different about everything. The lights went back on and Daisy blew out the candle. Lightening kept flashing outside the window and the storm brewed even louder.

But I barely noticed now. I couldn't get my mind off Aunt Melvinia. Suddenly there were so many things I wanted to know about her. And I couldn't stop wondering if Archie had made it home from the war or not.

We were all pretty quiet while we finished searching Aunt Melvinia's bedroom. We didn't find any boxes with Chinese writing on them, and we didn't find anything about Archie, either. When I glanced at my watch and saw it was two-thirty, we decided to search another room.

Daisy wiped the sweat from her forehead. "I think the attic is a good place to look next."

I hated to say it, but it didn't sound like a very good place to me. I pictured more dark spaces and lots more cobwebs. I remembered going to Aunt Melvinia's attic once when I was a really little kid. It was a scary place then, and I was sure it was still a scary place now. But I knew Daisy was right, and it was probably a good place to find the Ming.

The funny thing was, ever since we found out the Ming was a gift from Archie, I wanted to find it even more than before. Now I knew why it meant so much to Aunt Melvinia. It wasn't precious to her because it was so valuable. It was precious because it was a present from her husband who had been away at war.

And I was willing to do just about anything to find it and take care of it for her.

Even if it meant going into some spooky old attic.

"Okay," I told Daisy, "let's go up there."

"Yup," Hannah agreed. "I think we should search the attic, too. If I wanted to hide something, that's another place where I would put it."

So we were off again. I led the way down the hallway and up another flight of stairs. Then we had to open a door that led to some more very steep stairs.

Before we started to climb that staircase, I flipped on the light switch. Above us, the dark room became barely dim.

Like I said, it was a spooky old attic.

Daisy ran up the steps and Hannah followed her. I was the last one up the stairs, and the last one to step onto the wooden attic floor. I looked at all the furniture that was stacked around the huge open space. There were old chairs, tables, and dressers. There was even an old sewing machine. Plus there were lots of old trunks and boxes and books. And there were things like old skis and tennis rackets hanging from the wooden rafters.

Sure, I know, it sounds like a lot of stuff, but it wasn't nearly as cluttered as Aunt Melvinia's bedroom. That meant it was going to be a little easier to search.

On the other hand, her bedroom wasn't nearly as dark as this place was. And her bedroom wasn't half as noisy as this room was, either. With the wind howling outside, it sounded like we were in the middle of a hurricane.

Luckily, I knew Pinecrest never got real hurricanes.

The noise from the wind obviously didn't bother Daisy one bit. She had already sized up the huge space and was dividing up the duties. "Hannah, would you please look through those boxes by the wall? And Sally, would you please check those trunks over there?"

"Right-o!" Hannah said and sneezed.

"I'm on it!" I handed Hannah a tissue and then headed for the nearest trunk.

"Remember, girls," Daisy said, "we're looking for a wooden box with Chinese writing on it."

I tried to picture it in my mind. How hard could it be to find a wooden box with Chinese writing on it?

No matter how hard it was, I planned to keep looking until I found it. I was not going to let Aunt Melvinia down.

I tried to open the trunk in front of me, but the lid refused to budge. Okay, so I wasn't exactly off to a good start. But instead of wasting time, I just moved on to the next trunk. This time the lid came up, but it was a little heavy and it creaked and squeaked the whole way.

The first thing I noticed was the smell inside that trunk. It was kind of fresh and sweet smelling all at the same time. It reminded me of a closet where my mom kept things like sheets and towels.

I took a deep breath and started to look through all the old clothes and things stored away in that trunk. I pulled out a funny looking striped dress with an apron. The dress was really small at the waist, but it had a big full skirt. It was totally different from the flapper dress we'd found earlier.

I waved to Hannah to get her attention. "Hey, come take a look at this outfit!"

She skipped over, and I noticed there was a plastic nametag pinned to the apron. The top of the nametag said "Archie's Diner. " Just below that it said "Melvinia."

Hannah kneeled down beside me. "Oh, this is a classic 1950s dress. I love that era. It's one of my absolute favorites!" She pointed to the yellow dress she was wearing. "See? The dress I've got on is from the 1950s. The clothes were so awesome then! And I think the dress you're looking at was a waitress' uniform."

"A waitress?"

Well, I guess it did make sense. After all, the nametag pinned to the apron did say Archie's Diner. Did my Aunt Melvinia work in a diner? My very rich Aunt Melvinia, who didn't have to work a day in her life? That was the part that didn't add up.

Wowser! There was so much I didn't know about her!

But then something else hit me. The name of the diner. Archie's Diner. Was it named after Aunt Melvinia's husband, Archie? Did that mean he made it back from the war okay? I suddenly felt my heart start to pound inside my chest. It was strange, but now I wanted to know what happened to Archie just as much as I wanted to find the Ming.

Hannah pulled a framed, black-and-white photograph from the trunk. "Look! The name of the diner in this picture is the same as the name on the pin on that apron!"

I stared at the picture as Hannah held it up. It was a picture of an old-looking building and the sign on the roof said "Archie's Diner. " The building had big picture windows and you could see kids a little older than me sitting at booths inside. They were all drinking milkshakes from tall glasses with straws.

Standing in front of the building was Aunt Melvinia. She looked older than she did in the picture where she was wearing her flapper dress. But she looked a lot younger than she did when I knew her. In the picture, she was smiling and had her arms open wide. Like she was ready to give someone a hug.

I suddenly remembered the few times I had visited

Aunt Melvinia when she was a very old lady. She gave me a hug every time I saw her. For that matter, she was always so nice to me, too. Funny, I guess I didn't notice all that back then.

It's strange the things you notice when you grow up.

Hannah pointed to the building in the picture. "Your Aunt's diner looks just like a picture that my grandparents showed me. It was the diner they used to go to in the 1950s. That's where they had their first date. It was a really popular place to go back in the old days. All the high school kids went there after school."

"How fun!" I could just imagine it. Walking with friends to the diner after school. Then drinking sodas or milkshakes, and just sitting and talking.

Suddenly my thoughts were interrupted by a strange thumping noise. Hannah and I both glanced up to see Daisy at the far end of the attic. She had rolled up a rug that had been on the floor and now she was walking next to the wall. Well, actually, she wasn't really walking at all. She seemed to be doing some kind of strange dance step. She would put one foot in front of her, and then thump, thump, thump it on the floor. Then she'd put her other foot in front of her, and thump, thump, thump it on the floor, too.

Holy Cannoli! What was she up to now? Earlier I thought she might start dancing the Charleston. But this dance was like nothing I'd ever seen before! I couldn't imagine why she was dancing like that. And where did she get that flashlight?

Or maybe the question I should have asked was,

why did she have that flashlight? True, I could see she was shining the light onto the floor as she thumped along. But why she was doing this, I had no idea.

Then suddenly she stopped. She looked up at us and grinned. At that exact moment, I thought about climbing into the trunk and hiding. That's because I had a good idea she was about to say something I didn't want to hear. Something that meant going into more dark and spooky places.

Especially since I noticed she had started to toy with her beaded bracelet.

"I think I found a trap door!" she hollered above the whoosh of the wind that had picked up outside again. "Let's see where it goes!"

See where it goes? Couldn't we stay here and be happy just knowing it was there?

But I guess I already knew the answer to that question. Hannah and I dropped the dress and the picture into the trunk and raced over to help Daisy.

Daisy got down on her hands and knees and started to tug at something. I got on my hands and knees, too, and saw she was pulling at a thick metal ring. With my help, she pulled the ring so it stood upright. Then we both tugged on the ring even harder, so we could pull the trap door up. Finally, after lots of tugging, we had pulled up what looked like a square section of the floor.

"Wowser! How did you find this?" I stared at the dark open space.

"I had a hunch we might find something like this," Daisy said. "After we found the first secret passageway, I guessed there might be more in this house. So I just checked around the attic floor and then I found this trap door."

Hannah's eyes went wide. "Oh, maybe this whole house is full of secret passageways! Maybe you could go from one end of this mansion to the other through them."

That wasn't exactly the kind of house I ever wanted to live in.

"I was wondering the same thing," Daisy said. "Maybe we'll find out when we check out this secret passageway. I have a feeling it's important. Especially since we found Aunt Melvinia's bracelet in the other secret passageway." She shined the light from the flashlight into the dark opening in the floor.

I could barely see some rough wooden stairs below. "Where did you find the flashlight?" I figured if I got her to talk about something else, she might forget all about the new secret passageway.

"There was a metal box full of tools over there." With the flashlight, she pointed to the other end of the huge attic. "I found the flashlight right on top. I think it's really going to come in handy."

She shined the light back on the stairs. Then she took the first step down and started to take the second. "Sally, why don't you come with me and help me explore down here. And Hannah, would you mind staying up there and being a lookout? If Sloan Snodgrass shows up, be sure to shut the trap door. Then open it again when he leaves so Sally and I can get out."

Hannah nodded. "Sure, thing. You can count on me. I'll stand right next to the attic stairs and listen for him."

I wanted to suggest that I could be a very good lookout, and that maybe Hannah might like to go with Daisy. That was, until Hannah sneezed again. That's when I figured out why Daisy wanted me to go with her. Hannah's allergies were acting up with all the dust.

"Great. We won't be gone long." Daisy took another step down into the dark hole. "C'mon, Sally! Let's go see if that wooden box is in here somewhere."

That's when I found myself following my best friend down another set of dark stairs and then down another dark secret passageway. That's right, me, Sally Sosmart, a girl who gets scared even thinking about a scary movie, was walking straight into another dark, spooky place.

But I had to say, the whole thing wasn't nearly as scary with the flashlight. At least we could see the dusty wooden floor below us. And we could see the brick wall on one side, and a wooden wall on the other side. But there was no box with Chinese writing on it.

Ahead of me, Daisy asked about what Hannah and I had found in the trunk.

"It looks like Aunt Melvinia had a diner," I told her.

"Really? That's so amazing," she said.

As we stepped along, I filled her in about the picture and the waitress uniform. When I told her the name of the diner was Archie's Diner, she stopped dead in her tracks. She was quiet for a few seconds. Then she turned and said very softly, "Maybe

while we're searching for the Ming, we can find some
stuff about Archie, too."

"Wowser! That would be so great." I gave her
a quick hug.

Not only was she trying to help me find the Ming,
but now she was going to help find out about Archie,
too. That was so much more than I could ask for.
But I knew my best friend really well. Like I said
before, we're practically sisters. So I knew she wanted
to know if Archie came home from the war as much
as I did.

"I wish I could've met Aunt Melvinia," she said, as
she started to move forward again. "She must have
been such an awesome lady. I think I would've liked
her a lot."

"I know just what you mean." I smiled in the
darkness. One thing I knew for sure, Aunt Melvinia
would've really liked my friend, Daisy, the greatest girl
detective ever.

Without saying another word, we shuffled on
through the dark passageway. After what felt like
forever, Daisy stopped. She shined the flashlight all
around us. In front of us was a brick wall. It looked
like we had come to a dead end.

But that didn't make any sense. Why would
anyone put a secret passageway in a house if it didn't
lead anywhere?

Daisy took another step forward and shined the
flashlight to the right. "Just as I suspected," she said.

Huh? What did she mean by that? Before I could
say a thing, I saw the beam of the flashlight swing to
the right. Then half of it disappeared, like some giant

monster had swallowed it whole or something.

I gulped and grabbed onto Daisy's arm.

"This way," she said, like we were only at the mall trying to find our favorite store. I followed her and we took a right turn. I could see from the beam of the flashlight that the secret passageway kept going on.

Daisy flashed the beam of the light onto the floor. "Ah-ha! That's what I thought! This secret passageway connects to the one from Aunt Melvinia's bedroom!"

"How can you tell?" I peeked over her shoulder.

"See? Look at the disturbance in the dust on the floor!"

Okay, I'd heard her use that word before. It was the same word she used when she found my lost tennis shoe in my room this morning. It meant that something had disturbed the dust that always settles in a smooth layer.

And sure enough, when she shined the flashlight on the floor, I could see rows of smudge marks in the dust.

"What do you think caused that?" I asked her.

"Us."

"Huh?"

"We did," Daisy said. "Earlier today. When we came from the right, which would lead back to Aunt Melvinia's bedroom. Those are our footprints on the floor."

I suddenly got it. "Oh, from when we were shuffling along through the first secret passageway."

"Uh-huh," Daisy said. She kneeled down for a few seconds and took a closer look. Then she said,

"Okay, that's all I need to know for now. We'd better go back."

Words that were music to my ears.

I couldn't believe how happy I was to step up into the attic again. Earlier it had seemed like such a creepy place. But now, after wandering another secret passageway, the attic actually didn't look too bad. Funny how it worked that way.

Hannah was certainly glad to see us. "Oh, thank goodness you're back," she said as she bounced up and down. "I was starting to wonder if you two were all right." She helped me lower the trap door back into place. "I was so scared Sloan Snodgrass would show up. But while you were gone, I went through all those boxes and most of the trunks."

Daisy rolled the rug out across the floor, but she didn't cover the trap door. "Good job, Hannah! Did you find anything?"

Hannah shook her head. "Oh, I found lots of cool stuff, all right. But I didn't find the Ming."

I gave her a hug. "Thanks anyway." It was so great to have friends like Hannah and Daisy, friends who were there for me when I needed them.

"Maybe you two could help me open this last trunk," Hannah said. "I couldn't get the latch to work."

I knew the trunk well. After all, it was the first trunk that I had tried to open, too. The three of us kneeled in front of it and tried to figure it out.

After a few seconds, I heard Daisy say, "It's simple."

I should've guessed she'd say something like that.

"See?" she said. "The first latch isn't really the latch at all. It's hiding the real one." She slid the top latch out of the way, and sure enough, there was another one underneath.

She quickly unfastened the second latch and Hannah and I pulled up the lid of the trunk. It squeaked and groaned, just like the one I had opened earlier.

After we had pulled the lid open wide, we all glanced inside the trunk.

Suddenly I felt goose bumps crawl across my skin. My heart started to pound so loud in my chest that I thought it was going to explode.

For a few seconds, I couldn't speak. Neither could Daisy or Hannah. We all just stood there with our mouths hanging wide open.

Why?

Because, there in the trunk, fitting snugly between some blankets, was a wooden box with Chinese writing on it.

"What are you girls doing up there?" hollered a voice from the bottom of the attic stairs.

Sloan Snodgrass.

I heard his footsteps on the stairs. Any second now, he would be up in the attic with us.

Hannah and I both gasped. I thought for sure I'd never be able to breathe again.

"Not a thing!" Daisy yelled back. Then she slammed the lid back onto the trunk and slid the fake latch back into place.

Holy Cannoli!

CHAPTER 9

My heart was pounding so loud and so hard that I was sure Sloan Snodgrass would hear it. I put my hand to my chest, hoping I might make my heart quiet down a little. I huddled next to Daisy, and Hannah huddled next to me.

I'm sure my eyes must have been as big as my mom's dinner plates when Sloan Snodgrass finally stepped into the attic. Another man followed and stood beside him, so they completely blocked the stairs that led to the attic. The two men made a pretty strange looking pair. Sloan Snodgrass was skinny and wiry, and the other man was big and burly. The big guy reminded me of the bulldog who lived at my next-door neighbor's house.

I guessed this guy must be Sloan's friend, Eddie.
He smiled at us with dirty teeth. It looked like he
hadn't gone to the dentist in a long, long time.

But I couldn't smile back, even if I wanted to. I
was scared stiff. That's because I figured this man was
probably as mean as the bulldog who lived next-door
to me, too.

So, instead of smiling or saying anything, I just
stared at the two men. All the while, I couldn't stop
wondering what was going to happen next. Did these
men know we'd just found the box that was supposed
to hold the Ming? Or, if they didn't know, did they at
least suspect we'd found it?

If they did, that meant we were in big trouble.
Big, big trouble. After all, we'd already heard them
talking on the telephone about getting the Ming away
from us. No matter what they had to do.

And I, for one, didn't like the sound of that.

"Hello, girls," Sloan Snodgrass said in a sugary-
sweet voice. "This is my friend, Eddie. Say hello to
the little girls, Eddie."

I nearly jumped to the ceiling when thunder
boomed outside and the wind suddenly howled in a
high pitch. Luckily, I was hanging on to Daisy and
Hannah, or I would've gone like a rocket straight to
the rafters.

"Hello, little girls," Eddie barked in a gruff voice,
after the wind quieted down. He even sounded like a
bulldog. "Are you having fun up here?"

Fun? Was he kidding? I was too terrified to even
think about having fun!

"You girls have certainly been in this house for

a long time," Sloan said. His voice didn't sound as sweet as it did before. "It seems like you girls have been searching for a *ring* for hours. Have you found it yet?"

When he said the word "ring," he made the "r" roll, so it sounded like he said, "r-r-r-ring." Plus his eyebrows practically arched up to the top of his head when he said it. He was obviously putting a lot of emphasis on that word.

And you can bet we all knew why he was saying it like that. That's because he never bought our story that we were looking for a ring, and not a Ming. But he wasn't going to let on that he knew that we knew about the Ming.

Okay, I know it's kind of confusing, but let's just say the whole situation was really, really scary. Wandering around those dark secret passageways was nothing compared to this! The men in front of us were bad men, and they weren't exactly here to invite us out for ice cream.

I scooted closer to Daisy and pulled Hannah closer to me. I couldn't say a word. My voice was frozen. And I guessed Hannah's was, too, because she just kept making kind of a squeaking noise.

Holy Cannoli! If only we hadn't closed the trap door that led to the secret passageway. Then we could've had a quick getaway from Sloan and Eddie.

Daisy was the only one of us who could speak. "No, we haven't found the right ring," she said calmly.

And I mean, she said it *very* calmly. In fact, she sounded like she was only answering a teacher in class.

"We've been looking and looking and looking," she went on, "but . . . well . . . you know how us kids are." She paused and made the goofiest giggling noise I've ever heard.

What in the world was she up to now?

"I'm afraid I don't know what you mean," Sloan said. He started to tap his foot.

"Oh, you know," Daisy said, "we just get distracted. Since we're only kids, I guess we're just not very smart." She giggled in that goofy way again. "We started out looking for a ring. And then we thought, hey, maybe there's some cool stuff up in the attic. So, we came up here. And when we got here, we found so much great stuff to look at that we kept getting sidetracked." She giggled one more time.

I turned to stare at my friend. She had this grin on her face and looked as happy as she could be. Didn't she realize how much danger we were in?

She pulled my arm up and looked at my watch. "Oh, my, did you say we've been here for hours?" She smiled again at Sloan and Eddie. "I had no idea how much time had gone by. I guess we were just having too much fun. Especially since Hannah loves old clothes. And we've found lots and lots of old clothes for her to look at. Right, Hannah?"

Beside me, Hannah suddenly spoke up and started talking very, very fast. "Oh, yes! We found flapper dresses, and dresses from the 1950s. Those are my two most favorite eras! The clothes back then were so wonderful! Plus we found hats, and purses, and aprons, and pictures, and all kinds of fabulous stuff. I

could spend all day looking around this house. Aunt
Melvinia had the most wonderful things..."

"Yes, yes, she certainly did," Sloan interrupted and
tapped his foot even faster. "But remember, children,
you're here for a reason. Do you think you could get
back to the task at hand?"

Daisy waved her hand in front of her. "Oh, sure, I
promise we'll start looking for a ring again."

"Excellent. Would you kindly get back to work
immediately?" Sloan practically snarled.

"Absolutely," Daisy said. "Right after we find out
what happened to Archie."

"What?" Sloan's beady eyes went wide. "Archie?"

That's when it finally dawned on me what Daisy
and Hannah were doing. My friends were playing
dumb, to convince Sloan and Eddie that we hadn't
found the Ming. And as long as the men didn't think
we'd found the Ming, we would be safe. Just like
Daisy had told us earlier.

Wowser! I had such smart friends. Though I had
to say, when they wanted to play dumb, they sure
were good at it.

I decided it was my turn to get in on the act. "Oh,
my, oh, my, we really want to know about Archie," I
told the two men. "He was the love of Aunt Melvinia's
life! Isn't that romantic?" I fluttered my eyelashes
at them, just for effect. "Did you see the pictures of
Archie by his plane? He was soooo handsome! We're
positively dying to know more about him. Can you
tell us where we can find some stuff about Archie?"

"Please?" Daisy added with a big smile. "Then
after that, we promise we'll start looking for a ring

again."

Sloan stared at Daisy. "I believe you'll find some information about Archie in the study on the first floor."

Daisy clapped her hands like it was the best news she'd heard in a million years. "Oh, thank-you, thank-you, thank-you!"

Sloan didn't take his eyes off her. "Do you promise you'll look for a ring as soon as you're finished there?"

"Oh, yes," Daisy practically shouted. "We'll start looking just as soon as we're finished finding out about Archie!"

She turned to look at Hannah and me. "C'mon girls! Let's zoom!"

She grabbed my hand, and I grabbed Hannah's hand. Then she pulled us in the direction of the attic stairs, which were still being blocked by Sloan and Eddie.

I suddenly wondered what she was doing. After all, we weren't exactly big, huge football players who could tackle these men. Even though Sloan was small, he was still a whole lot bigger than any of us. And Eddie was gigantic. Even if all three of us girls tackled him, we didn't stand a chance.

But apparently Daisy hadn't even considered that. Instead she ran directly at Eddie and shouted, "Excuse me!"

I couldn't believe what happened next. Eddie simply moved out of the way and let us go right on by. I was so surprised, I nearly tripped down the attic stairs.

Daisy tugged us along behind her until we had flown past the final step and landed in the hallway. That's when she didn't have to pull us along anymore. That's because the three of us broke into a dead run. We didn't stop until we'd run down the hallway, then down the stairs, and finally the other hallway that we'd run down earlier. We turned in to the study, which was right across from the room where my cousin Jewell had been stealing jewelry.

None of us said a word until we were standing safely inside the study.

"Holy Cannoli!" I looked at Daisy and Hannah. "That was a close one! I thought for sure something bad was going to happen up there."

"Me, too." Hannah bounced up and down. "That big guy was even scarier than Sloan Snodgrass! I really didn't like the way he smiled at us, because his eyes looked so mean. Those men sure want Aunt Melvinia's Ming, and they'll do anything to get it. Anything." Hannah gulped.

Daisy glanced at the hallway. "I think we're safe for the moment. They don't think we've found the Ming yet. And I think they want us to find it for them. They must think we know something they don't."

"And we do." I hugged myself to keep my arms from shaking. "We found that box with the Chinese writing on it."

Daisy started to pace back and forth across the wooden floor. "Yes, we did. But I think we fooled them for the time being. They don't know we found that box."

Now I felt my toes start to tremble. "But as long

as they're watching us, how will we ever get that Ming out of the attic? And once we get the Ming, we're all going to be in danger."

Hannah's eyes were wide. "Oh, my gosh! What are we going to do? We've got to get that Ming, but we can't let those men hurt us!"

"Well, girls," Daisy told us. "Like I said before, I've got a plan."

Thank God for that, I thought.

Daisy glanced at my watch again. "Sally, do all the kids related to Aunt Melvinia get to pick something from her house?"

I shrugged. "I think so. But I don't think all the kids were interested. My brother and some of my boy cousins could have cared less."

"Good," Daisy said. "I'm going to run out and find Holmes, now. But while I'm gone, I want you and Hannah to find a decoy."

"Huh? A decoy?" What was she talking about? I always thought a decoy was a wooden duck that hunters used in duck hunting. Surely Daisy didn't want us to find a duck.

Daisy pointed to the bookshelves all around the room. They were overflowing with stuff, just like in Aunt Melvinia's bedroom. "Look for a box that looks sort of like the one with the Chinese writing on it," she said. "Then I want you to find some pottery to put inside it. Something that might look like a Ming. Just do your best."

I smiled at her. That's because, for once, I had figured out her plan. "Oh, I get it. We're going to fool Sloan and Eddie into thinking we already found the

Ming. That way they won't find the real Ming."

Daisy smiled back at me. "Uh-huh. That's part of my plan."

"But wait," Hannah said. "Won't we be in danger if those men think we've got the Ming?"

"Not if they think we don't have it," Daisy said.

"Huh?" I looked at her cross-eyed. What in the world did she mean by that? How could we make Sloan and Eddie think we had the Ming and make them think we didn't have the Ming at the same time? Once again, I wasn't sure what planet my friend was on.

Before I could ask anything else, my great girl detective friend ran into the hallway and waved at us. "I've got to hurry," she said. "I'll be back really soon." And then she was gone.

Hannah and I just stood there looking at each other. I was dying to know what Daisy was up to, and I guessed Hannah probably was, too. But we both knew our friend well enough to know there was no use trying to figure it out.

We would just have to wait.

Hannah and I both shrugged, and then we glanced around the room.

"I guess we'd better hurry up and find a decoy," Hannah said. "Daisy could be back really quick."

"I hope so." I took a good look at all the stuff in the shelves. "There's got to be something here that we can use," I told Hannah. But for the life of me, I couldn't spot anything that looked like an old Chinese vase.

Beside me, Hannah let out a cry and pointed

directly in front of us. "Over there! On the desk!
Between those piles of papers and things! It's a blue
pottery vase. It's a perfect decoy for the Ming!"

She didn't have to tell me twice.

We both ran to the desk. Sure enough, wedged
between stacks of papers, boxes, and other stuff was
a blue vase. But since I'd never seen a Ming before,
I had to take Hannah's word that it would make a
good decoy.

We pulled the vase up off the desk. As soon as
we did, one of the stacks of stuff caved into the empty
spot where the vase had been.

Hannah's blue eyes practically danced. "This vase
is perfect! Now all we have to do is find a box and
we've got a great decoy!"

I smiled at her and started to pile the stuff back
into place. That's when something caught my eye.

"What's this?" I pointed to a little box that was
in the middle of the mess. I pulled it out to take a
closer look.

The box was made from dark leather and kind of
looked like a flat jewelry case. There were two rows
of gold zigzags around the edges, and in the middle,
there was some kind of writing in gold. The only
problem was, the letters were nearly worn off and the
top was pretty scratched up. No matter how hard I
tried, I couldn't make out the words.

Hannah set the vase down and stood beside me.
"I'm not sure what that is, but that box looks kind
of familiar."

Suddenly I felt goose bumps race across my skin.
For some strange reason, I was scared to open that

box. Wowser! We'd already found one diamond bracelet. Could there be another one inside this box?

Hannah squinted her eyes. "I wish we could read those gold letters. That first letter looks like a 'P', but I can't tell about the rest . . ." Her mouth dropped open and she looked at me.

"The WREB!" We practically shouted at the same time.

It only took me about a half a second to pull my invention from my pocket. Then I held it right over the box and turned it on. It whirred quietly, just like it was supposed to. A few seconds later, I could see the writing perfectly.

I read it out loud for Hannah. "It says, 'Purple Heart.'"

She gasped. "Oh, no!"

"What's the matter?" I didn't know why, but my voice came out like a whisper.

"A Purple Heart is for soldiers who got hurt," she whispered back.

"Huh?" I put the WREB back in my pocket.

She pointed at the box. "Open it. I'll show you."

I carefully grabbed onto the front of the case and pulled the lid up. And there, inside the box, was a medal, the kind soldiers wear.

But this one was a lot prettier than any medals I'd ever seen. It had a purple ribbon with a purple heart at the bottom. The heart had gold around the edges and a sideways face of a man in the center.

I looked at Hannah who now had tears in her eyes. Why was she so upset?

"It's from World War Two," she said. "I've seen

those in my mom and dad's store. They only gave Purple Hearts to soldiers who got injured. It was a very great honor and it meant the soldier was very brave. That medal must have been for Archie."

I thought my own heart was going to stop beating. Now I knew why Hannah was so upset. Archie must have been injured in the war.

"But wait a minute," I said. "If they gave Archie this medal, he must have come home."

Hannah shook her head. "Not necessarily. If the soldier died, then they gave the Purple Heart to the soldier's family."

"Oh." I felt tears sting my eyes. I closed the little box and put it back on the desk.

Hannah and I both took a step back.

"I don't like the looks of this," I sniffed.

"Me, either," she said.

"We still don't know if Archie came back from the war or not." I pulled some tissues from my pocket. I handed her one and used the other to dry the tears on my cheeks.

Hannah wiped her own eyes. "Nope. We still don't know what happened to him."

All at once I started thinking about Aunt Melvinia. It must have been so hard for her when the war was on. She was probably at home, just waiting and wondering if Archie was coming back. It must have been awful.

Aunt Melvinia must have been very, very brave. If only I could be as brave as she was. I knew I could start by rescuing her Ming, even though the whole situation seemed very scary.

Hannah must have felt the same way I did. "We've got to save Aunt Melvinia's Ming," she said. "We can't let Eddie and Sloan steal it."

"No, we can't," I agreed. "Let's hurry up and find a box to put that vase in, just like Daisy wanted us to."

Hannah blew her nose and pointed up at some bookshelves. "Look," she said. "Behind that big potted palm tree. I see a box that's almost the same size as the one we found in the trunk."

I leaned over to take a closer look. Sure enough, she was right. It was a wooden box that was about the right size. Unfortunately, it was way up on the top shelf.

"I'll grab that chair behind that desk," Hannah said.

While I tugged and tugged at the potted palm tree, until it finally moved, Hannah scooted the chair over. Then she butted it up against the bookshelves. Because I'm taller than she is, I climbed on the chair and stood up.

But I couldn't stop thinking about the Purple Heart. And I couldn't stop thinking about Archie and Aunt Melvinia as I reached for that box. I stretched up as far as I could, but the shelf was still too high. I could barely touch the bottom of the box.

"Here," Hannah said. "Try standing on these books." She pulled out three large books and stacked them on top of each other. Then she pushed the books against the back of the chair, and held them in place with her hands.

Holy Cannoli! I took one look at that setup and

I knew it was going to be trouble. Everybody knows it's not safe to stand on things that are stacked on something else. I thought of all the stuff I had stacked all over my room. Those piles were always falling over. Stacks of stuff are never very sturdy.

But what choice did I have? I had to be brave. And I was willing to do just about anything to protect Aunt Melvinia's Ming.

But hopefully that didn't mean risking my very own neck.

I took a deep breath, just like I'd seen Daisy do a million times to get her courage up. Then I stepped onto the chair. So far, so good. I leaned forward and grabbed onto one of the lower shelves. I used it to steady me while I stepped up onto the stack of books.

Wowser! I couldn't believe how high I was!

I let go of the shelf and reached up slowly with both arms. At long last, I could grab the bottom of the wooden box. Now all I had to do was take the box off the shelf and bring it down with me.

No problem.

I got a firm grip, and slowly, carefully, tried to pull the box from the shelf.

But it refused to budge!

Next, I tried wiggling the box from side to side, but it still stayed stuck. I sighed and closed my eyes for a minute. Maybe if I gave it one more really, really hard tug, I might get it to move!

I opened my eyes again. No matter what, I had to get that box down, so we could use it for a decoy. So we could keep Sloan and Eddie from getting Aunt Melvinia's Ming. So I could protect the precious gift that Archie had given her.

I took another really, really deep breath. Then I tugged and tugged and tugged, with all the strength I had! Suddenly, I felt the box start to slide free.

Hannah yelled, "Watch out! The books are moving!"

But it was too late.

I felt the books beneath me slide out of place. And that's when I felt myself falling, falling, falling backwards.

Straight into the potted palm.

That's when I heard the voice that made my skin crawl.

"Hello, Ferret Face," it said. "Hope you had a nice trip. Good going. You killed that plant!"

I closed my eyes and groaned. At that moment, I wished the potted palm was really a huge Venus Flytrap that would swallow me up. Then I wouldn't have to face the person I'd been hoping to avoid all day.

I sighed and turned to look at him.

It was my brother. Scare'em Aaron.

CHAPTER 10

I wanted to scream. Holy Cannoli! Why, oh, why did Scare'em Aaron have to show up at that exact moment? Why did he step into this very room just in time to see me tumble into the potted palm?

Now I'd never hear the end of it. And when I say I would never hear the end of it, I wasn't kidding. Scare'em Aaron lived to torment me. He loved it, and he was really, really good at it.

Worst of all, according to my mom, because I am five years older than he is, I wasn't supposed to tease him back. According to her, I am supposed to act more mature, and not stoop to his level. That meant I wasn't allowed to fight fire with fire, if you get my drift. My mom's advice was to ignore him so he would just give up and quit teasing me.

Fat chance. It seemed like the more I ignored him, the more he tried to annoy me.

Wowser. I sure wish someone would write a handbook on how to handle a rotten little brother like Scare'em Aaron. I'd be the first one to read that book.

Or maybe I could invent a machine that would turn a nasty little brother into a nice kid. Big sisters everywhere would thank me.

Unfortunately, I didn't have any of those things to help me out at the moment. I was going to have to face Scare'em Aaron without the aid of any books or machines.

I pulled myself up out of the plant and dusted the dirt off my behind. I wasn't sure which looked worse — me or the plant.

While my brother laughed and pointed, Hannah rushed over to me. "Oh, Sally! I'm so sorry. I never should've told you to stand on those books. It's a good thing that plant was there to break your fall. Are you all right?"

I smiled the best I could. "I'm fine, I think." I wiggled my toes and legs, just to make sure everything was still working like it should be. The truth be told, the only thing that was smarting was my pride.

I pointed to the wooden box that was sitting on the floor, not far from the plant. "At least I pulled the box down."

Hannah gave me a quick hug. "You did great. Now we'll have the perfect decoy for Daisy's plan."

She went to retrieve the box while I glared at my

brother.

"What are you doing here?" I demanded. "I've got some really important things to do at this house. You can't be bothering me." I spoke in my best I'm-a-lot-older-than-you voice.

"Hey, Ferret Face!" He scrunched up his nose at me. "Daisy asked me to come here."

"Daisy did what?" I could hardly believe it. Why would my best friend set me up to be tormented by Scare'em Aaron? She knew how I felt about him.

Aaron put his hands on his hips. "That's right. She had Holmes come to our house to get me. When I got here, Daisy said she had a special mission for me. She said it was important. So there!" He said the word "mission" with a whole lot of emphasis, like he was some kind of secret spy or something.

I rolled my eyes, and tried to pull the leaves of the palm tree back into place. But it was useless. It looked like I had flattened the poor plant permanently.

I turned around just in time to see Daisy practically fly into the room. She took one look at me, and her eyes went wide. Then she glanced at the crushed plant and at the chair by the shelves, where the books I'd been standing on were all messed up. Next she looked at the wooden box that Hannah was holding and finally, she looked back up at me again.

"Sally, are you all right?" she asked. "Wow, that box was way up in those shelves! Did you hurt yourself when you fell into that plant?"

I should have known my detective friend would figure that one out. "I'm okay," I told her. "No permanent damage."

"Thank goodness." She nodded at the wooden box. "You and Hannah found a perfect box. After we put some Chinese writing on it, it'll look just like the one we found in the attic."

Now it was my turn to figure out what she was up to. "Is it true? Did you really ask my brother to come here?"

She smiled at Scare'em Aaron. "Yup, I did. And he was nice enough to agree."

Nice? Did she say nice? Now I began to wonder if there was something seriously wrong with my friend.

Sometimes it's hard for me to believe it, but Daisy doesn't mind having my brother around every once in a while. That's probably because she always wished she had a brother or sister of her own. I don't think she's crazy about being the only kid in her family.

But she might change her mind in a hurry if she had to live with my brother every day. There are many, many days when I would happily trade places with her. The weird thing is, my mom claims I'll learn to like my brother when we're both grown-ups. Somehow, I just can't imagine it.

I looked over at Scare'em Aaron, who was grinning at Daisy like he'd found the true love of his life. I had forgotten the little weasel had a crush on my best friend. How embarrassing. But at least he was usually on his best behavior in front of her. Apparently, he was trying really hard to impress her.

Maybe that's why he agreed to help her with this "mission," as he put it.

"So, what did you want him for?" I asked Daisy.

She grinned at me. "Aaron is going to help out with my plan."

"Huh?" I looked from Scare'em Aaron to Daisy, and then back again. My little brother stuck his tongue out at me.

Just as I was about to return the favor, Hannah held up the blue vase. "Daisy, look at this! You wanted a decoy for the Ming, and boy, oh boy, did we ever find a good one!"

Daisy's dark eyes sparkled. "Wow! You girls did such a great job! Let's get that vase packed up in the box. We've got to hurry! Before I came back to the study, I spied on Sloan Snodgrass and Eddie in Aunt Melvinia's bedroom. They're exactly where I want them."

Daisy grabbed some old newspapers and I took the lid off the wooden box. She bunched up the newspapers and put them on the bottom of the box. Then Hannah carefully put the vase inside. Daisy put more newspapers around the vase, but she still left it pretty lose inside the wooden crate.

I put the lid back on. "Why do you want those men to be in Aunt Melvinia's bedroom?"

Daisy ran to the desk and found a big black magic marker. "They're in the perfect position for my plan to work. And Holmes is in place, too."

She opened the lid on the magic marker and started drawing on the wooden box. But before long, I saw that she wasn't really drawing at all. Instead she'd made marks that looked kind of like Chinese writing, just like we'd seen on the real Ming box.

"Perfect!" Hannah bounced with excitement. "It

looks like the one we found in the attic."

Daisy stood back and took a good look at her work. "Let's hope it's enough to fool Sloan and his friend, Eddie."

Then she handed the wooden box with the vase inside to my little brother. "Now, Aaron, remember, I want you to wait outside the front door with this. Just like we talked about. The storm is over and the sun is out, so you won't have to worry about lightning, or anything."

"Daisy, I don't know if that's such a good idea," I said. "I mean, I'm not exactly crazy about my brother . . . But, wowser, I don't want him to get hurt, either. I don't want Sloan and Eddie to go after him."

Daisy shook her head. "Don't worry. I don't want him to get hurt, either. That's why I've got Holmes in on this, too. And there will be so many witnesses that Sloan and Eddie wouldn't dare harm a single hair on his head."

My brother gave me a nasty look. "Hey, Ferret Face, don't be such a big baby. I won't get hurt, so don't even think about trying to boss me around. I'm going to help Daisy whether you like it or not."

I had to clamp my jaw shut really tight to keep from saying anything nasty back to him. At that moment, I wanted to do a *whole* lot more than just boss him around. Sometimes it's really hard to be the mature kid in the family.

"Okay, everyone," Daisy said. "Here's the plan."

We all gathered around close so we wouldn't miss a word of what she said.

"Everyone will be stationed in a different part of

the house," Daisy said. "Hannah, I want you to be stationed at the bottom of the stairs. I will be stationed in the hallway that leads to the front entry. I will be hiding, but I'll still be able to see you from where I'm standing. Aaron will be stationed just outside the front door."

I was just about to ask where I would be stationed when Daisy turned to me. "Sally, you've got a very important role in this plan," she said.

Holy Cannoli! Did she say an important role for little old scaredy-cat me? My heart started pounding like a bass drum. I held my breath while I waited to hear what she was going to say next. Obviously, she had me confused with someone who is very, very brave.

Daisy looked directly at me. "Sally, I want you to lure Sloan Snodgrass and Eddie from Aunt Melvinia's bedroom to the front door."

"Huh?" I could hardly believe my ears. Now I was sure my friend was on another planet! "You want me to do what?"

"It'll be easy," Daisy said. She smiled like our teacher does when she tries to convince us that we can solve a really hard math problem. "All you have to do is pretend like you're going to the bedroom to look for something. Act casual. Then mention that your brother picked his one item from the house and that he's going out the front door. Then say something about how your mom will like the vase your brother got. That's all you have to do."

"That's it?" I felt my heart start to slow down a little. "But I still don't understand how that will get them to the front door."

"Don't worry," Daisy said. "After you tell them what I told you to say, that's exactly where they'll go."

Daisy turned to Hannah. "When you see the men start to come down the stairs, I want you to signal me."

"Got it," Hannah said. "I'll wave to you."

"Good," Daisy answered. Then she looked at my little brother. "Aaron, I don't want you to start running until you see me, okay?"

He smiled up at her. "Whatever you say, Daisy."

She nodded at him. "Good. And you know what to do after that, right?"

"You bet," he answered. "Just like we talked about when I got here."

"That's it," she said. "Your mission is very important, you know. I'm counting on you."

"I won't let you down, Daisy," he said in a voice that reminded me of my dad. He puffed his chest out as far as it would go. If he hadn't been holding the box with the vase, I'm just sure he would have flexed his arm muscles next.

Ugh. What a little showoff! How embarrassing can one little brother be?

Daisy looked at me and then at Hannah. "After Sloan and Eddie have run past you two, I want you to meet me at the front door. I don't want any of us to be in the house when this is all over."

"But wait," Hannah jumped in. "Shouldn't we grab the Ming first before we leave?"

"Nope," Daisy answered. "They'll see us with it. We'll have to come back for the Ming. I've got a plan to get it out so that Sloan and Eddie won't know a thing."

Another plan? Wowser, my friend Daisy sure knew how to come up with good plans. At least, I hoped they were good plans.

I figured I was about to find out soon, since Daisy was waving us all toward the doorway. "Now, if everyone does their part," she said, "this plan should go like clockwork! C'mon everybody, let's go!"

She ran down the hallway and we all ran after her. We kept running until we reached the staircase. Then Hannah stood at the bottom of the stairs, just like she was supposed to. Daisy and my little brother ran to the hallway that led to the front entry. I saw Daisy point my brother in the direction of the front door and then she ducked behind a wall. A few seconds later, I saw Daisy poke her head out. She gave us the "thumbs up" sign.

That meant everybody was in place. Everybody but me, that is. And now it was time for me to do my job.

Wowser, was I ever scared. I didn't like the idea of facing Sloan and Eddie by myself. Especially since I knew they were bad men who would stop at nothing to get that Ming.

I started to climb the stairs very, very slowly, taking just one step at a time. Before I knew it, my teeth had started to chatter. And after I climbed a few more steps, my knees began to knock.

Holy Cannoli! How was I ever going to pull off my part in Daisy's plan if I was too scared to move?

But I couldn't let her down. She'd already told me

my role was really important. Because, if I couldn't get those men to go to the front door, Daisy's plan wouldn't work at all.

Besides that, Scare'em Aaron would never let me live it down. It was just my luck that he was being so brave and not even batting an eyelash at his part in Daisy's plan. But me, well, that was a different story altogether.

I stepped onto another stair and grabbed onto the railing. I had to go through with my part. I had to be brave, if not for me, then for Aunt Melvinia.

I suddenly thought of my Aunt Melvinia. She must have been so brave while she waited to hear about Archie and if he was coming home from the war. Then I thought of Archie, too. He must have been very, very brave to even fight in the war.

If they could be brave, then so could I. I had to go through with what Daisy had asked me to do. But hopefully I would come out in one piece, and not end up with a Purple Heart myself.

I took a deep breath, just like I'd seen Daisy do a zillion times. Then I ran up the rest of the stairs. It was like diving into a cold swimming pool — sometimes it's just best to get it over with.

I got to the top of the stairs and ran down the hallway to Aunt Melvinia's bedroom. I stopped in the open doorway and spotted Sloan Snodgrass and Eddie right away. They had taken everything out of Aunt Melvinia's closet, and boxes were stacked everywhere.

Both men turned to look at me.

"Yes, what is it?" Sloan asked in a voice that came through his nose.

I was all out of breath and could hardly speak. Especially since my teeth were still chattering. "My brother," I said. "He wants something from this room at the front door is his item with my mother's vase."

Whoops! That wasn't what I was supposed to say. Sloan and Eddie both walked toward me.

Holy Cannoli! I really messed that one up! Now how was I going to get them to the front door?

CHAPTER 11

Sloan Snodgrass stared at me with his beady little eyes as I stood in the doorway of Aunt Melvinia's bedroom. He and Eddie kept coming closer and closer. I wanted to run, but my knees were knocking so bad I wasn't sure I could even stand up much longer. So running was definitely out of the question.

Besides, running away was probably a bad idea anyway. After all, I had a job to do. And if I didn't hold up my end of the bargain, well, the rest of Daisy's plan would fall apart. Then where would we be? We'd never get Aunt Melvinia's Ming. Or, at least, we'd never get it without being in danger from Sloan and Eddie.

That meant I had to do my part of the plan.

There was no sneaking out of it.

Sloan stopped about two feet from me and put his hands on his hips. "What did you say, little girl?"

Okay, it was time for me to deliver my line again. And this time I had to get it right. On top of that, Daisy told me I was supposed to act casual, probably so the men wouldn't guess what we were up to. But how was I supposed to act casual when I was scared out of my mind?

I wondered what Daisy would do at this moment. Thankfully, the answer came to me right away. I faked a yawn. Daisy told me a long time ago that people who yawn are either bored or tired. And people who are bored or tired don't look very suspicious. In other words, they look casual.

So I faked a gigantic yawn. I opened my mouth wide and stretched like a bear coming out of hibernation. I did a pretty good job, if you ask me. It was enough to make Eddie yawn, too.

Then I smiled at the men. "I said, I just came back to Aunt Melvinia's room to look at her hats again. And my brother found his item that he wants to take from the house." I paused for effect and looked at my fingernails. "In fact, he's just headed out the front door now. Wowser, my mom sure is going to be happy with that vase he found."

Sloan's eyebrows arched up and I thought his eyes were going to pop out of his head. He let out kind of a scream and took off running. Eddie looked a little confused, but he ran right after Sloan.

Holy Cannoli! Daisy was right! That's all I had to say to make those men run to the front door.

I skipped down the hall and ran down the steps after them. Wowser! Did those men ever run fast!

Hannah was waiting at the bottom of the stairs for me, and together we ran behind the two men. We followed them out the front door.

Daisy was already outside. The sun was shining brightly again, and she was standing at the corner of the huge porch. She was waving to my brother who was standing next to Holmes. Holmes had both the passenger car door open, and his driver's door open. The funny thing was, he already had the car running.

My little brother waved back at Daisy. Then he pulled the blue vase out of the wooden box for a few seconds. It was just long enough for Eddie and Sloan to spot it. That's when things got really interesting!

Sloan and Eddie started shouting, "No! It's the Ming! Don't let them get away!" They ran for the car. As soon as they did, Scare'em Aaron jumped into the backseat and Holmes slammed the door. Then Holmes shouted, "Can't wait! Gotta go!" He jumped into the driver's seat and slammed his own door.

Sloan and Eddie almost reached the car when Holmes sped away and made the tires squeal like a racecar driver! Holy Cannoli! I've never seen him drive like that before!

All the while, Daisy and Hannah and I jumped up and down like cheerleaders, yelling, "Go! Go! Go!" Of course, we weren't yelling at Sloan and Eddie, but for Holmes to get out of there.

Sloan and Eddie chased the car for a few feet and then finally stopped running. Eddie shook his fist in the air. Sloan fell onto the ground and started whining like a little puppy. I could hardly believe a grown man could act like that. Even Scare'em Aaron doesn't act *that* bad!

A few seconds later, Sloan jumped up and started screaming at Eddie. Then Eddie started to yell back. The men's voices got louder and louder, and if you ask me, they sounded pretty scary.

That's when I felt Daisy take my hand. She grabbed Hannah's hand, too, and pulled us across the wide stone porch. She didn't stop until she had pulled us around to the other side of Aunt Melvinia's mansion.

Even though we couldn't see the men, we could still hear them yelling at each other. They went on for at least five minutes, until I heard Sloan shout, "Those little girls did this! It's all their fault! They snuck that Ming right out from under our noses!"

Then I heard the front door slam shut hard! It made kind of an echoing noise all around the house.

Even though I know it was scary and everything, I couldn't help but giggle a little. After all, we had completely fooled Sloan and Eddie. We had tricked them into believing the Ming was already gone, when it was really safe and sound in the attic. Now I finally understood Daisy's plan.

I was about to tell her what a good job she had done when I noticed she was toying with her beaded bracelet.

But wait a minute. That didn't make sense. Everyone knows that Daisy plays with her beaded bracelet right before she finds an important clue. But since we'd already found the Ming, what clue was left to find? Surely she hadn't stumbled onto another mystery, before we even finished solving this one!

Just then I heard a very scratchy voice say, "Would you girls please not stand in the petunias?"

We all turned to see a man walk around the back corner of the house. He was a tall, skinny man with hunched shoulders. He had gray hair that curled out from under a big straw hat. He must have been about as old as Aunt Melvinia had been, but his brown eyes sparkled like a young kid's.

"I just planted them flowers a few days ago," he said in the same scratchy voice. "And if you wouldn't mind, I'd appreciate it if you didn't stand in the flowerbeds. The storm was a little rough on them, but this sunshine will make them perk up right nice."

I looked down at my feet. Sure enough, we were standing in a patch of pink, purple and red flowers. Wowser, with all our running around, I guess we hadn't noticed the flowers.

Hannah was the first to speak up. "We're so sorry, sir. We didn't see these pretty flowers, but we'll move right away."

I followed Hannah and Daisy as we carefully tiptoed out of the garden so we wouldn't hurt the plants.

"I'm sorry, too," Daisy said. "By the way, I don't think we've met. My name is Daisy Diamond. And these are my friends, Sally Sosmart and Hannah Hystory." She glanced at me and then at Hannah.

The old gentleman grinned. "Ah, it's right nice to meet you, little ladies. The name's Phineas

Philodendron. I am Aunt Melvinia's gardener. Or, at least, I was, until she passed away. I'm going to miss her terribly. Even so, I plan to keep the place looking nice until it's all sold off. She would have wanted it that way."

I stepped closer to the man. "You knew Aunt Melvinia?"

"Oh, yes," he smiled. "Known her for years. Let's see, if your last name is Sosmart, you must be her kin then."

"That's right! We were related." I suddenly felt my heart pounding inside my chest. I didn't know why, but there seemed to be something very special about this man. Maybe he could tell me more about my Aunt, and about Archie as well. I was just dying know about her life and the people in it.

"Did you know Aunt Melvinia very well?" I asked him.

"Oh, my heaven's, yes. I knew her as well as anybody. Of course, I didn't meet her until after the war was over. That's when she was running her diner. Archie's Diner, she called it."

"We saw pictures of it up in the attic," Hannah jumped in. "It looked like it was such an awesome place!"

"Oh, it were, little lady," Phineas said. "It was all shiny with pink and turquoise chairs when it was brand new. I'll never forget the first time I went there. You could walk in at lunchtime and smell the soup cooking, or the pies baking. Best smell in the world, if you ask me. Your Aunt Melvinia could bake an apple pie that made your mouth water just thinking about it. She was the best cook I ever met."

I could hardly believe my ears. "She was?" I had no idea that Aunt Melvinia was such a good cook.

"Oh, yes, ma'am," Phineas went on. "Melvinia could make pretty darn near anything. She were real talented, that one. The funny thing was, all her high society ladies laughed about her diner."

"They did?" I asked.

"Why?" Hannah wanted to know. "It was such a great little place. And her waitress outfit was wonderful."

"I'll bet I know why," Daisy said. "Her friends probably didn't understand why she was working so hard at the diner if she already had lots of money."

Phineas smiled at her. "You got a good head for figuring out people, young lady. It'll take you a long way in life. And you're right. But Melvinia was a very kind-hearted soul. She didn't want to just rattle around in her mansion and live a spoiled life. No, she wanted to get out and do something. And what most people don't realize is, she helped lots and lots of people with her diner."

I felt my eyes go wide. "She did?"

"Oh, yes, ma'am," Phineas went on. "She knew when people were down on their luck. And she probably gave away more meals than she ever got paid for. She gave meals to poor people at lunch and dinner."

His eyes sparkled as he went on. "Then the teenage crowd came in after school. If Melvinia knew a kid came from a poor family, she always made sure that kid left with a full belly. Best of all, she was always real quiet about it, so nobody got their pride hurt. Whether they could afford it or not, everyone got to eat a hot meal at a booth in her diner, with silverware and everything."

"What a kind lady," Hannah said. "She must have been wonderful."

"You got that right," Phineas went on. "And I'm proof of it. I got injured in the war, and couldn't make a decent living for a while. Melvinia made sure I got fed, and then she even gave me this job here. Weren't none kinder than Melvinia. In her own quiet way, she saved lots and lots of people from ruin. Most people don't know it, but she was kind of a town hero."

Holy Cannoli. I had no idea. I stared down at the flowerbed for a moment, just to think about all the things that Phineas had said. It was funny, I'd known Aunt Melvinia all my life, but I guess I'd never really known her at all. When I was a little kid, I thought Aunt Melvinia was a boring, old lady.

Turns out I couldn't have been more wrong. Wowser! I never knew about all the cool things she had done in her life. I hate to admit it, but I guess I never took the time to find out. In a way, that made me feel really sad.

Okay, it was time for me, Sally Sosmart, girl scientist and inventor, to make some serious changes in my life. So I made a silent promise to myself. I decided to learn as much about other people and their lives as I could. Especially older people. There were probably lots of interesting people around and I didn't even know it.

I had learned so much from Aunt Melvinia's life

this afternoon. That meant there must be other people out there that I could learn even more stuff from. You know, important things. Things about how to live your life. And how to be a good person.

Suddenly, I thought about Archie. He must have been a good person, too.

I looked back up at Phineas and blurted out the question that had been bugging me all afternoon. "What about Archie?"

"Yeah," Hannah said. "Did Archie make it home from the war?"

Phineas pulled off his straw hat and bowed his head. "I never met Archie," he said in a quiet voice. "But I'm told there weren't a finer gentleman in all of Pinecrest."

"Did he . . ." Daisy started to say and then bite her lower lip.

"No," Phineas said. "He never made it home from the war. His plane was shot down in the Pacific. He died after he saved four of his crewmen. He was a very brave man."

We all bowed our heads for a moment.

It wasn't the news we'd been hoping to hear. We all wanted to believe that Archie had made it home. We wanted to believe that he and Aunt Melvinia had lived happily ever after.

I heard Hannah sniffle a little bit, and I saw Daisy holding back tears. I felt like crying, too. How sad for Aunt Melvinia. No wonder she named her diner after him.

Hannah was the first to break the silence. "We found a Purple Heart in the study," she said quietly.

"It must have been for Archie."

"That's right, little lady. Archie was given a Purple Heart. It's a very great honor for any soldier. I got one myself, but at least I'm here to talk about it. I'm afraid a lot of the folks I served with aren't. During the war, people made sacrifices that were very, very hard."

My eyes blurred with tears as I thought about Archie. I remembered the letter we'd found under Aunt Melvinia's pillow, the letter that Archie had written her. It was probably the last letter Aunt Melvinia ever got from him. No wonder she kept it under her pillow.

That also meant the Ming must have been the last Christmas present she ever got from him, too. That's why it meant so much to her.

"What about the Ming?" I asked Phineas. "It must have been very important to Aunt Melvinia."

Wowser! Was I ever surprised by what happened next.

Phineas suddenly plopped his hat back on his head and his face crinkled up in anger. "Oh, yeah, you can say that again! Except that's one name I never want to hear again!"

Then, much to my surprise, he stomped off.

I looked at Daisy and then at Hannah. "What did I say?"

"Beats me," Daisy said with wide eyes. "But that sure was a strange reaction."

"Very strange," Hannah said. "Maybe Phineas is looking for the Ming, too. Or maybe he hoped Aunt Melvinia would leave it to him in her will."

Once again, Daisy started to play with her beaded bracelet. "I don't know," she said, "but something sure upset him. I'd sure like to know what."

She stared in the direction that he had stomped off. Then she stared at the flowerbed for a few minutes. She walked over to the edge of the dirt and squinted her eyes as she examined it.

"Hmmmm . . ." she said. She kneeled down for a moment and took a good look at the soil.

As usual, I wasn't sure what planet my friend was on.

I was about to ask, but then she turned to look at Hannah and me. "We'd better get going," she said. "We've got to get that Ming out of the attic."

"But how?" Hannah wanted to know. "If we go through the front door, Eddie and Sloan will see us."

"Yeah," I added. "And it sounded like they were pretty mad at us. I don't want to run into those two again."

"We won't have to," Daisy said with a grin.

"Huh?" Hannah and I practically said at the same time.

Daisy pointed to the side of the house. "While you two were looking for a decoy for the Ming, I found another way to get into the house."

Okay, now she'd really lost me. Did she really think we were just going to walk through walls?

I stared at the place where she was pointing. "Um, Daisy, I hate to break it to you, but there's no door there."

"Of course, not. Not a door that you can see, anyway." She tiptoed carefully through the flowerbed again.

For some strange reason, I just followed her like I was a cocker spaniel or something. "What do you mean?"

Hannah came along, too. "Oh, I get it," she said.

I glanced at both my friends. "Would someone mind explaining it to me?"

"Sure," Daisy answered. "I found the place where the secret passageways in the house end up outside. We're going to go through the secret passageways to get to the attic. That's how we're going to get the Ming out."

Holy Cannoli! Did she say more secret passageways?

CHAPTER 12

Okay, you guessed it. A few minutes after Daisy told us how we were going to get the Ming out, there I was. I went shuffling down yet another secret passageway, following Daisy and Hannah. Holy Cannoli! I'd been through so many secret passageways in one afternoon that I was actually getting used to it. It hardly even scared me anymore.

Okay, maybe I was a little scared. Maybe you could even say I was really scared. But at least I wasn't totally terrified like the first time I went through a secret passageway in this house.

It helped a lot that Daisy had brought the flashlight with her again. She had opened the secret wooden panel on the outside of the house, and we climbed up a bunch of stairs to get to the first dark passageway. Of course, we pulled the door tight behind us, so nobody would figure out what we were up to. We didn't want Sloan and Eddie to find that door open and then follow us.

And so far, the going had been good. We'd carefully shuffled along in the darkness, with only the flashlight to guide us.

Before I knew it, we came up on the vent in the wall where we could see into one of the downstairs bedrooms. It was the same bedroom where we'd first seen my cousin, Jewell, stealing jewelry.

Ahead of me, I saw Daisy put her finger to her lips, giving us the sign to be quiet. Then she switched off the flashlight and we stood there in complete darkness.

That's when I heard the voices coming from the other side of the wall. It was Sloan Snodgrass and Eddie. And one thing was for sure, they were mad!

Sloan's whiney voice rang through loud and clear. "I can't believe they got out with that Ming! Those rotten little girls. I knew I should never have trusted them! My life shall be ruined now."

"Those nasty kids," Eddie said. "I can't believe they fooled us."

"Oh, yes, you've got that correct," Sloan said. "They fooled us, all right. They tricked us out of a priceless Ming. This was my one chance in a lifetime to get one, and now . . . Now . . ." Sloan quit talking and let out a loud, sad cry, kind of like a dog howling at the moon.

Hannah and I jumped, and I nearly screamed.

Luckily, I put my hand over my mouth and squelched any noise that wanted to come out.

"If only they would come back into this house," Eddie said. "Then we could get them!"

"Yes," Sloan said. "If they'd come back inside, we might have something to work with. But no doubt, they're a million miles from here now."

"Yeah," Eddie agreed. "They're probably back home. All safe and sound."

Now I had to hold back a giggle that tried to come out. I thought it was pretty funny that these men thought we were long gone. Little did they know, but we were just a few feet away in a dark, secret passageway. Wowser, we really had them fooled!

"Too bad," Sloan went on. "Otherwise we could possibly trick them into bringing the Ming back. After all, they're only children, and we're the grown-ups. Surely, we could find some way to outsmart them."

Fat chance. There was no way they could outsmart us! Once again I had to hold back a giggle. After we got the Ming out, I would have to sit down and have a really good laugh!

"We wouldn't have to outsmart them," Eddie replied. "All we'd have to do is kidnap them. It would be easy. We could hold them for ransom until that old driver brought the Ming back to us. Then we could let them go."

"You idiot," Sloan said. "We'd get caught. It wouldn't do us any good if the driver knew we were the kidnappers."

"We could do it secretly. Like make a phone call and disguise our voices. Or send the driver a note or something."

"Hmmm . . ." Sloan said. "Maybe it could work."

All of a sudden I didn't feel like laughing anymore. These awful men were talking about kidnapping us! I scooted closer to Hannah and Daisy. Then we grabbed each other's hands and held on tight!

"Yeah, kidnapping," Eddie went on. "That's a great idea. We could have a secret drop-off place for the Ming. Then they'd never suspect it was us."

Suddenly I felt goose bumps jump to attention on my skin.

"Good plan, Einstein," Sloan yelled. "But you've forgotten one very important point!"

"What's that?"

"Those little girls aren't here anymore!"

"If they were," Eddie said, "we could get them!"

Suddenly I heard a noise that made me jump about a mile. A loud voice beside me sang, "Your mom wants you to go home at six. Your mom will ground you if you're late. It's five o'clock. You've got an hour left. Don't be late, or your mom will ground you for a week."

Holy Cannoli! It was my singing watch! I'd forgotten that I'd set the alarm for five o'clock!

I tried to put my finger on the turnoff button to make the thing be quiet. Unfortunately, Hannah and Daisy also jumped for my watch, probably trying to shut off the alarm, too. As they tried to help me, they actually prevented me from reaching the button. So my watch continued to sing, "Your mom wants you to go home at six. Your mom will ground you . . ."

And so on.

My heart was pounding really loud and hard by the time I finally hit the turnoff button. At last the watch went quiet. But my heart didn't quiet down one bit.

Wowser! Had Sloan and Eddie heard my watch? And if so, would they figure out that we were still in the house somewhere?

I felt Daisy tug Hannah and me away from the vent in the wall. We moved slowly and quietly along the dark passageway, about ten feet from the vent. Then I felt her tug us down. Quietly, we followed her lead and crouched down on the floor.

I heard Sloan Snodgrass shout, "What was that?"

Eddie said, "I dunno. Something about your mom grounding you."

"It's those girls!" Sloan practically screamed. "They're here! In this house! I just know it."

His voice kept coming closer and closer. The next thing I knew, I could hear his voice coming from the vent in the wall.

Holy Cannoli! Would he figure out that there were secret passageways in this house? And if he did, would he come and find us?

"Where are they?" Eddie asked.

"I don't know," Sloan answered him. "But they're somewhere in this house! Let's find them! If we work this out, then the Ming will be ours. Hurry!"

"But where do we look for them?" Eddie asked again.

"I don't know," Sloan yelled. "Just find them!"

Okay, I've got to say, I wasn't too tickled to hear

all that. My arms started shaking and my legs started shaking. And before long, my whole body started shaking. I could barely stand when Daisy pulled us up and started us moving down the secret passageway again.

After we had gone about twenty feet, she switched on the flashlight again. "We've got to get that Ming out of here in a hurry," she whispered to Hannah and me. "We can't stay in this house much longer!"

She didn't have to tell me twice! I followed along at breakneck speed as we jogged down the passageway. Then we took a flight of stairs and then a right. Wowser! There sure were a lot of secret passageways in this house!

At long last, we went around a corner to the left. Then, a few minutes after that, I noticed a long set of stairs that led up to a trapdoor.

I recognized that trapdoor. We were at the attic!

I didn't know whether to cheer or to hide. Getting to the attic meant we were close to getting the Ming out.

But it also meant we would have to leave the safety of the secret passageway. We would be easy prey for Sloan and Eddie.

Daisy climbed up the stairs until she could touch the trapdoor above us. We followed and stood beside her.

Then she switched the flashlight off. "Shhh . . . Let's be quiet for a minute and see if we can hear Sloan and Eddie."

We all stood silently in the dark for a few minutes, listening for any noises.

"I don't hear anything," Hannah finally said.

"Me, either," I told them.

"Okay," Daisy said. "Let's hurry. Help me lift this trapdoor up a little bit. Then we'll listen again and see if we hear Sloan and Eddie."

We all stepped up to the next stair, so we could reach the trapdoor better. Then we pushed up on it. Luckily, it didn't make any squeaking sounds as we slowly raised it up a little.

"Do you hear anything?" Daisy whispered.

"Nope," I whispered back.

"All quiet," Hannah whispered, too.

"Good," Daisy said softly. "Now let's get this door open and get the Ming."

With the three of us pushing, the trapdoor went up very easily. When it was halfway up, Daisy ran out and grabbed the top end. Then she brought it back to the other side of the floor and let it land very softly. And very quietly.

"Good," she said, still talking just above a whisper. "The coast is all clear. Now, we'd better walk on tiptoes so nobody can hear us."

So we did. It seemed like it took ten years to move across that attic floor. I can't tell you how many times I was dying to just break into a dead run! But my friend Daisy had a good point. We had to be very, very quiet so Sloan and Eddie wouldn't hear us.

Plus, as a girl scientist, I can tell you that things always sound a lot louder in a room below. Even if we didn't think we were making much noise up in the attic, it would be a lot louder below us. Sound just gets magnified that way.

So we tiptoed and tiptoed. Finally, we made it to the trunk where we'd found the wooden box with the Chinese writing on it.

"Let's listen for Sloan and Eddie again," Daisy whispered to us.

Hannah and I both nodded "yes."

I can't remember ever being so excited or so scared in my whole life. The only thing that stood between us and that Ming was a big wooden trunk with a trick lock.

After we were sure Sloan and Eddie weren't on their way up to the attic, Daisy quickly worked the lock. She had it unlocked in a matter of seconds, and she started to lift the lid. Then Hannah and I helped her pull the trunk lid up slowly, so it wouldn't squeak.

But just as we got the lid up all the way, it let out a loud "errack!"

We all froze in place. Hannah and Daisy and I looked at each other with wide eyes. It seemed like we had all suddenly stopped breathing, we were so quiet. I listened for Sloan and Eddie, and I'm sure my friends were doing the same thing.

Luckily, we didn't hear a thing.

We all breathed a huge sigh of relief.

Then Daisy reached down and pulled up the box with the Chinese writing on it.

I felt a wide smile cross my face. This was it. Aunt Melvinia's Ming. I'd been waiting for so long to see it, and now that moment was almost here.

"Open it," Hannah whispered. She looked like she wanted to bounce up and down, but I knew she was forcing herself to stay still.

"Yeah," I whispered. "Let's open it. It'll be too dark to see it in that secret passageway."

Daisy did as we asked. She carefully pulled the lid off the wooden box. Inside, there was lots of straw-like stuffing.

Daisy immediately started to dig through the stuffing, until she pulled up one little cup with Chinese designs on it. Then she pulled out a second cup. They looked a little like teacups, but without the handle.

Next, she pulled out an entire teapot.

I could hardly believe it. Wasn't the Ming supposed to be a vase?

Hannah's mouth went wide. "Wait a minute," she whispered. She picked up one of the cups and looked on the bottom. "This isn't a Ming."

"Keep looking," I told Daisy. "Maybe the Ming is still in there."

Daisy pulled out a few more little cups. Then she said, "There's nothing else in here."

"This is nothing but a tea set," Hannah told us. "It looks like it's probably from the 1940s. My mom and dad have one in their shop."

"No Ming?" I whispered.

Daisy shook her head. "That's all that was in the box."

Hannah's eyes were wide. "And those things are definitely not Mings."

I could hardly believe it. So that was all that had been in that wooden box. A few little cups and a teapot. I felt my mouth fall open.

Daisy and Hannah and I all stared at each other. Holy Cannoli! If the Ming wasn't in this box, then where was it?

CHAPTER 13

"We'd better get out of here," Daisy said. She put the cups and the teapot back into the wooden box. Then we all helped to close the trunk lid, and Daisy refastened the lock.

We weren't about to wait around and try to figure out why the Ming was not in that box. Not with Sloan Snodgrass and Eddie hot on our trail.

Together, we all tiptoed across the attic floor again. Then we quickly went through the trapdoor and pulled the cover on tight.

Daisy switched on the flashlight and plopped down on the steps. "I need a moment to think," she said softly. Even by the light of the flashlight, I could see how sad she looked.

Wowser. For hours now, we thought we'd already found the Ming. We were so sure it was in the box with the Chinese writing. But it wasn't. So it turned out, we hadn't really found the Ming at all.

I guess I wouldn't be honest if I said I wasn't feeling pretty bad right about now. More than anything, I wanted to take care of that Ming for Aunt Melvinia. That's because I knew how much it meant to her.

But now it looked like we were sunk. We hadn't found the Ming, and we couldn't exactly run around the house looking for it anymore. That's because Sloan and Eddie believed we had already taken it. And they were just itching to grab us and hold us captive until Holmes brought the Ming to them.

The only thing was, Holmes wouldn't have anything to bring as our ransom, since he didn't really have the Ming.

I know, it's all very complicated. But the bottom line was, since Sloan and Eddie were after us, we couldn't wander around the mansion. That meant we couldn't search for the Ming out in the open. To make things worse, it was already after five o'clock, and my mom wanted me to leave for home by six.

We were running out of time.

Tears filled my eyes. I felt like I had failed Aunt Melvinia. And the last thing I wanted to do was let her down.

But somehow I didn't think Aunt Melvinia would see it that way. Somehow I think she would be proud of me for trying so hard to find the Ming, and for being so brave. She would also be proud that I had such good friends. And believe me, it was at moments like this when it really paid to have good friends.

Hannah said, "What are we going to do? I don't like the looks of this at all. If we don't find the Ming, Sloan and Eddie will find it eventually. Especially after they finish getting everything ready for the auction. Then I'm just sure they'll steal it."

I pulled out a tissue and blew my nose. "I know, I know. It's true. If only there was something we could do."

Just then I looked down and saw Daisy toying with her beaded bracelet. My breath caught in my throat. Was Daisy about to find another clue?

Maybe we weren't sunk after all!

"Daisy," I said carefully. "What is it? What are you thinking about?"

Her eyebrows crinkled. "What do you think caused those little dugout places in the flowerbeds?"

"Huh?" I could hardly believe my ears. "I guess I never really looked at it," I told her. I felt my heart sinking in my chest. This wasn't a good time for my friend to be on another planet. We needed her here on earth right now.

"The storm," Hannah answered. "The storm could've made a mess out of the dirt."

Daisy shook her head. "I don't think so. Rain might cause some erosion, but not little holes like that. Did anyone else notice that nasty smell?"

Wowser. Daisy must have been more upset about not finding the Ming than I realized. Why else would she be talking about dirt and smells in the garden instead of finding the Ming?

Before I could say another word, she jumped up. "Let's go!" she practically hollered.

"Go?" I felt my eyes go wide.

"Where?" Hannah asked.

"To Aunt Melvinia's bedroom!" Daisy shined the flashlight down the stairs and into the secret passageway.

Then she took off running. Hannah and I ran to keep up with her.

"But, why?" I asked in a loud whisper.

Hannah whispered loudly, too. "Yeah, Daisy, why?" She covered her nose with a tissue, just in time to catch a sneeze.

"Because," Daisy said, "I think I know where the Ming is."

Wowser! Did I hear her right? Did she really know where the Ming was? I crossed my fingers and prayed she was right. Not only was time running out, but Sloan and Eddie were still after us, too. It would be a miracle if we found the Ming and all got out of the house in one piece.

It took us only a few minutes to arrive at the door that led to Aunt Melvinia's bedroom from the secret passageway. The secret door was built into the wall paneling that matched the rest of the paneling in the bedroom. But on this side, it just looked like a large piece of wood.

"Okay, everybody," Daisy said. "We have to find the device that opens the door from this side."

"Oh, that's right," Hannah said. "Last time, we opened this door from inside the bedroom by twisting the wall sconce. So there must be a different way to open it from this side."

I slid my hands around the door and felt for a handle or something. "I wonder what it looks like."

"It could be anything," Daisy said. "We'll know when we find it." She shined the flashlight against the walls, and on the ceiling and the ground.

Hannah moved her hands all over the brick wall, trying to find a way to open the door. "Maybe you can only open this door from the other side," she said.

Daisy shined the flashlight directly on the door now. "I sure hope not. Otherwise, one of us is going to have to go up to the attic and down the regular stairs to this bedroom."

My legs began to shake at the thought of that! If any of us went running around through the mansion, we'd be an easy target for Sloan and Eddie. That meant we just *had* to find a way to open this door! And fast.

We searched and searched, for what felt like hours. We practically slid our hands over every inch of the door, and the walls, too.

"Maybe there's a loose brick," Hannah suggested. "Sometimes in the movies, somebody pulls out a loose brick and the secret door opens."

"Good idea," Daisy said. She shined the flashlight on the brick wall, while Hannah and I felt for any bricks that might wiggle.

But after several minutes, we hadn't found a single loose brick.

"All right," Daisy finally said. "I'm going to go back up to the attic, and out the trapdoor. Then I'm going to sneak down to the bedroom and open the secret panel door from the other side."

Huh? Was she kidding? I wasn't going to risk letting my best friend get caught by Sloan and Eddie.

I leaned against the paneled door. "No way. If you go, so do I. We'll be safer if there are two of us."

"I'm going, too," Hannah jumped in. "I'm not letting you girls face those bad men by yourselves."

Daisy smiled at us. "Thanks, girls. But it's better if just one of us goes. You two stay here. If they catch me, you two can run for help."

"I don't want you to go," I told Daisy.

And I meant it. I didn't want anything bad to happen to my best friend. I stepped over to give her a hug, so she couldn't go anywhere. But when I did, I felt something tug at my tennis shoe. So instead of giving her a hug, I tripped right into her.

Luckily, Daisy and Hannah caught me as I fell forward.

"My shoe's stuck," I told them.

Daisy instantly shined the flashlight down at the floor. Sure enough, my shoelace was caught on a metal object, about the size of one of my mom's big serving spoons.

"Way to go, Sally!" Daisy practically shouted. "That's got to be the device that opens the door."

"You found it!" Hannah cheered. "It's a metal lever." She leaned over and freed my stuck shoelace. I stood up and turned to look at the metal object. It was so dull and dark, that it blended in with the wood floor.

Wowser! Sometimes the things you're looking for are so close that you trip right over them.

Could that be the case with the Ming?

Daisy held her finger to her lips to signal that we should be quiet. "Let's listen to make sure Sloan and Eddie aren't in Aunt Melvinia's bedroom."

We stood there in complete silence for a few minutes. Listening. But we couldn't hear a thing from the other side of the wall.

"Okay," Daisy said. "Let's zoom."

She shined the flashlight onto the floor and stepped on the metal lever. The door slowly began to open.

In a few seconds, we could see right into Aunt Melvinia's bedroom. After being in that dark passageway, we all squinted in the light.

The room looked a lot different from when we'd been searching in it the first time. Sure, there were piles and piles of stuff everywhere. But during the afternoon, Sloan and Eddie had added to those piles by taking things out of the closet and drawers. Now the room was a bigger mess than it was before.

Daisy was the first one to jump into the room. "Hannah, would you mind being a lookout? Just stand by the door and warn us if you hear Sloan and Eddie coming."

"Got it!" Hannah skipped to the door and flattened herself against the wall. Then she stared into the hallway.

Daisy turned to me. "I want you to help me search. I'm looking for the stack of framed photographs that I looked through when we first got here."

"I'm on it!" I glanced around the room. "Where

were the pictures when we were here before?"

She pointed to the right side of the bed. "Over there," she said.

I felt my eyes go wide. That part of the room was positively piled high with all kinds of junk. It was going to take forever to get through it. And we didn't exactly have that much time.

But we weren't going to give up either. We both ran over and started picking up boxes and moving them to the center of the room. After a few trips, we'd gotten the pile down enough that we could actually see some of the floor.

"Over there," Daisy pointed. "I can see a frame!"

We both practically jumped at the picture that was sticking out. But before we could reach the rest of the pictures, we had to move more junk out of the way.

So we tugged at newspapers, and ornaments, and books and all kinds of stuff. A few minutes later, we had cleared enough room for Daisy to look at the whole stack of framed photographs.

Just then, Hannah yelled, "They're coming. Run! Get back into the secret passageway!"

Hannah practically flew around all the boxes and went straight through the opening in the wall. I was just a few seconds behind her. Gee, I never thought I'd be happy to be inside a secret passageway. But for once, I was.

I got ready to step on the lever to close the door, when I realized that Daisy hadn't run into the passageway with us. Where was she?

I looked out into the room and spotted her. There

she was, flipping through the pile of pictures just as fast as she could!

"Daisy," I yelled in a loud whisper. "Get in here! Sloan and Eddie are coming!"

"I'll be right there!" she said. "I've almost found it."

Just then, Sloan and Eddie burst into the room. They came to a halt just a few feet from the door that led to the hallway.

This time, I was sure my heart had stopped beating altogether. I couldn't breathe. I felt Hannah grab my arm with shaking fingers.

"Well, well, well," Sloan said in a very nasty voice. "What have we here? If it isn't the little girls who are too smart for their own good."

"Yeah," Eddie said. "We didn't like the way you tricked us before. Now we've got a little trick for you."

Holy Cannoli! Somehow, I figured their tricks weren't the kind that made you laugh! In fact, I guessed we wouldn't think their tricks were very funny at all.

CHAPTER 14

If I told you I was scared at that exact moment, well, let's just say that would be the understatement of the year. It would be like saying my brother, Scare'em Aaron, is just a little bit of a pest. That's because Scare'em Aaron is a *major* pest.

And well, I was about as terrified as one girl could be at that moment. My arms were shaking and my legs were shaking and my teeth were chattering, too.

I stared across the room at the men who now blocked the door to the hallway.

Sloan Snodgrass stared back at me with his beady little eyes. "You two girls come out of that closet," he said. Then he nodded at Daisy. "And you put those pictures down. If you girls come along nicely and don't give us any trouble, you won't get hurt."

149

Holy Cannoli! Was he kidding? I had no intention of going along with him "nicely," as he put it. That's because I didn't believe him for a second! After all, we'd already overheard his conversation with Eddie, where they talked about kidnapping us. I knew what they had in store for us, and it wasn't good!

To top it off, I had no idea why he wanted Hannah and me to come out of some closet. After all, we were just standing inside the secret passageway, not a closet.

Then it suddenly hit me. Sloan and Eddie hadn't figured out that Hannah and I were standing in a secret passageway. The passageway was dark, so, while they could see us, they couldn't see past us. To them it probably looked like we were standing in a closet.

That's when I knew we had a chance to get away from them! And when Eddie started to walk toward Daisy, like he was going to grab her, I felt something stir inside me. It was a new feeling. I wasn't just scared anymore. I was mad.

And there was no way I was going to let that rotten man kidnap my best friend! I suddenly thought of Archie, who had saved some of the men who were shot down in his plane in the war. He must have felt the same way that I did right now.

I pushed Hannah behind me and yelled to Daisy, "Run!"

She grabbed one of the framed photographs and ran for the entrance to the secret passageway.

Eddie immediately ran for her, and she pushed

some boxes over to slow him down.

"Hurry, Daisy!" I yelled again.

That's when things got tricky. I knew that once Daisy got into the secret passageway, I had to close the secret door to keep Sloan and Eddie out. The only problem was, the door closed very slowly. So if I waited for Daisy to get inside, Eddie would be able to get through, too.

That meant I had to start closing the door so that Daisy had just enough room to get through. But I had to time it so that the door would be fully closed by the time Eddie got there.

Tricky, huh?

I watched Daisy run toward me. When she was only a few feet away, I stepped on the lever to close the paneling door. The door slowly started to turn into place. I watched my best friend squeeze through just in time.

But the door wasn't fully closed yet. Through the small opening, I saw Eddie make a dive for the door, like a baseball player diving for a base.

Just before the door closed all the way, Eddie reached his big arm through the opening. From the floor, he managed to hold the door so it couldn't close shut.

"I've got it!" He yelled to Sloan. "I'll pull this open and we can get those girls!"

Fat chance. This was one day when no one would be kidnapping me or my friends. I looked at Eddie's big arm on the floor, as he tried to pull the door back open.

Then I lifted my foot and took a deep breath.

With every ounce of strength I had, I stomped on Eddie's arm just as hard as I could.

Eddie screamed and pulled his arm out, and the door snapped tightly shut. My friends and I cheered and screamed in the darkness.

"Good job!" Daisy yelled.

"You saved us, Sally!" Hannah said.

Holy Cannoli! You know what? They were right. I did save us. And I have to say, I was really proud of myself for doing that. Somehow I had a feeling Aunt Melvinia and Archie would have been proud of me, too.

We hugged each other like we hadn't seen each other in a hundred years.

Then we heard Sloan and Eddie pounding on the door and yelling at us.

"We'd better get out of here," Daisy said.

"Would you please turn on the flashlight?" Hannah asked.

"I can't," Daisy answered. "It's back in Aunt Melvinia's bedroom. I didn't have a chance to grab it before we ran out. We're going to have to find our way in the dark."

"No problem," I heard myself say. "We've been through here enough times that we should remember the way."

Wowser! Did I really say that? Me, who was so terrified the first time went through a secret passageway?

Well, I guess that's the fun part about growing up. You learn all the things you can do but didn't think you could do when you were younger.

I know, it's complicated, but you'll know what I mean when it happens.

Maybe that meant there was hope for Scare'em Aaron after all.

We shuffled through the secret passageways pretty fast, and before we knew it, we were outside again. We carefully tiptoed through the flowerbed and then stopped on the grass.

There was no sign of Sloan and Eddie, so we figured they were still back in the house.

By now, I was dying to know what picture Daisy had grabbed. And I was also dying to know what it had to do with the Ming.

Before I could ask, she pulled Aunt Melvinia's diamond bracelet from her pocket. She looked it over carefully.

"Ah-ha!" she finally said.

"What is it?" Hannah and I asked at the same time.

"Just as I thought," Daisy answered. "See these tiny black hairs caught in this bracelet?"

I stared at the place where she pointed. "Uh-huh."

"I see them," Hannah said, too.

"Well," Daisy said. "Those hairs don't belong to your Aunt Melvinia."

"Nope," I told her. "She had gray hair."

"That's right," Hannah agreed.

I tried to put the pieces together in my brain. "So, you're saying this bracelet didn't belong to Aunt Melvinia?"

"It did and it didn't," Daisy answered.

Hannah crinkled her eyebrows. "How is that possible?"

"Because this bracelet isn't a bracelet," Daisy said with a grin.

Okay, once again my friend was clearly on another planet. She wasn't making sense at all. I could tell by staring at the piece of jewelry that it was definitely a bracelet. How could Daisy think it was something else?

Hannah asked the question that I was thinking. "If it's not a bracelet, then what is it?"

"It's a collar," Daisy said. "That's why we found it in the secret passageway."

I could hardly believe my ears. "A collar?"

Daisy held up the framed photograph that she had grabbed from Aunt Melvinia's bedroom. "Here. Take a look at this."

I grabbed the picture, and Hannah and I both stared at it. Inside the frame was the photo of the face of a beautiful black cat with huge gold eyes.

"Take a look at the cat's neck," Daisy told us.

I pulled the picture closer so Hannah and I could see it better. Sure enough, though it was mostly hidden by the cat's fur, we could barely make out the edges of a sparkly diamond collar.

"Does that mean . . ." Hannah started to say.

"Are you telling me . . ." I began to ask.

"Let's look on the back of the picture to be sure," Daisy answered before we had even finished our questions.

She took the picture and turned it over. Then she removed the back of the frame and pulled the picture out.

She held the back of the picture upward, so we could all see it. There was some writing there, but the ink had been smeared.

"If only we could read it," Hannah said. "I wonder what it says."

Then we all looked up at each other. "The WREB," we all shouted together.

It took me half a second to pull my invention from my pocket. I turned it on and heard the familiar whirring sound that told me it was working perfectly. I was dying to see what that writing said.

But instead of reading it myself, I decided to let my friend, Daisy, have the honor. After all, she had been the one to uncover these clues. And she and Hannah had both been so nice to help me. They had risked their own necks to help me search for the Ming and honor Aunt Melvinia's dying wish.

I passed my WREB to Daisy. "Here. You read it."

She grinned at us and then held the WREB over the back of the picture. Then she read the words aloud. "The cat who has brought so much sunshine into my life," she read. "My precious Ming."

Holy Cannoli!

CHAPTER 15

I flopped down onto the green grass of Aunt Melvinia's yard. "You mean, the Ming is a cat?"

Daisy nodded. "Uh-huh. It looks like it."

Hannah's eyes were wide. "It's not pottery?"

"Nope. Not this time," Daisy said.

I stared at the photo again. "So, all along, Aunt Melvinia wanted me to take care of her cat?"

"Yup," Daisy answered.

Wowser! I could hardly believe it. All this time we were searching for pottery, and it turned out we were on nothing but a wild goose chase. Or maybe I should say, a cat chase.

Now I looked around the yard. "But where is the cat? I mean, Ming?"

I noticed Daisy was toying with her beaded bracelet again. For once, I couldn't have been happier.

"That's the last part of the mystery," Daisy said. "But I have a good idea where we can find out. After all, we already heard what Phineas the gardener said about Ming. He said that was a name he didn't want to hear again. I have a hunch that's because Ming was digging in his flowerbeds."

"Oh, that makes sense," Hannah said. "So if we find Phineas, maybe he can tell us where Ming is."

"That's right." Daisy jumped to her feet. "But we've got to hurry. We don't have much time left!"

She motioned for us to follow and we all took off running to the back of the house. In a matter of minutes, we found the gardener in the back, clipping some rose bushes.

"Excuse me, please," Daisy said, just a little out of breath.

The old man smiled at us. "Yes, little ladies. How can I help you?"

Daisy smiled back at him. "We were wondering if you knew what happened to Aunt Melvinia's cat."

"Oh, heaven's, yes. That thing was a real pest! It kept digging up my flowerbeds. What a mess he made! Using my gardens for his catbox! Why Melvinia was so crazy about that critter, I'll never know. Anyway, I got rid of it."

For a second, I could barely breathe. "What do you mean, you got rid of it?"

"Oh, I took it to the animal shelter this morning. I figured they'd find a good home for the big guy.

Maybe somebody else won't mind him digging in their garden."

"Thank-you," Daisy said quickly. Then she turned to me. "Sally, what time is it?"

I glanced at my watch. "It's twenty till six," I told her.

Daisy's dark eyes went wide. "C'mon! We've got to hurry! I'll bet the animal shelter closes at six! We've got to get there before it closes."

My heart started to pound really hard inside my chest. "Let's run to my car. Holmes should be back from dropping Scare'em Aaron off at my house."

"Let's zoom!" Hannah agreed. "We've got to get Ming!"

We waved goodbye to Phineas and ran as fast as we could to find Holmes and the car.

He was practicing his violin when we came running up.

All three of us started to shout at once, so I guess it was probably pretty hard for him to understand what we were saying. I finally signaled for my friends to be quiet. Then I said, "Please take us to the animal shelter. We need to get there before it closes."

Holmes put his violin back in the case. "Didn't you pick your item from the mansion, Ms. Sally?"

"Not yet, Holmes," I told him. "But I'll explain along the way."

We all jumped in the car and in a matter of minutes, we were on the way to the animal shelter. I explained the whole story to Holmes and asked him to drive as fast as he could. For once, I noticed he was driving just a little above the speed limit.

I sat back and looked at my friends. Then I started to get really, really nervous. "If Phineas took Ming to the shelter this morning, do you think someone has adopted him already?"

"Let's keep our fingers crossed," Hannah said. "I'll bet Ming is there just waiting for us."

"Me, too," Daisy added. "He's probably only been there for eight hours at the most. That means the odds are good that no one has adopted him yet."

I sure hoped my friends were right. More than anything, I wanted to take care of Ming for Aunt Melvinia. I would just die if somebody else already took him home.

It seemed like it took hours and hours for us to get there. It was three minutes till six when we pulled up to the Pinecrest Animal Shelter.

Daisy, Hannah and I practically flew out of the car the minute we arrived. Holmes followed behind us.

We ran in the front door, which thankfully, was still unlocked.

A lady with long brown hair greeted us at the front door. "Hello, girls," she said with a smile. "I'm afraid you'll have to come back tomorrow. We're just closing for the night."

"Please," I said. "Just give us a few minutes."

"We're looking for a black cat named, Ming," Hannah jumped in.

"He was brought to this shelter by mistake," Daisy added.

"That's correct," Holmes suddenly spoke up behind us. "Apparently, it was a dying woman's last wish that the animal be taken care of by young Ms.

Sally Sosmart here. It would mean a great deal if these girls could find the cat and bring it home."

The lady smiled again. "I'm afraid we can't adopt an animal to children."

Holmes bowed to the woman. "I shall sign and take full responsibility, Madame."

"Very well, then," the lady said. "But I'm not sure if the cat you're after will still be here. We had a lot of adoptions today."

"Please," I pleaded with the lady. "Please just let us take a look."

The lady sighed. "All right. Follow me, then. I'll give you just a couple of minutes. Then I have to close up." She stood up and led us to some swinging doors that led to the room with the animal cages. Inside that room, we saw all kinds of cats in cages. And much to my surprise, there were lots of black cats there, too.

"Oh, no," I moaned. "How will we find Ming?"

"That's easy," Daisy said. "I'll bet he knows his name."

And the next thing I knew, Daisy started calling, "Here, Ming! Where are you, Ming?"

Hannah and I joined in, too. "Here, Ming!"

We slowly walked past the rows and rows of cages, waiting for a cat to answer us.

And sure enough, around the corner and on the other side of the room, we heard a cat meowing loudly. We all ran over to find a cage on the bottom row. And there, right in front of us, was a big black cat with huge gold eyes. His fur was so shiny it reminded me of the patent leather shoes I had when I was little. The cat looked exactly like the picture that Daisy had found in Aunt Melvinia's room.

I kneeled down and put my fingers against the bars of the cage. "Are you Ming?" I asked the cat.

He answered with a meow, and rubbed his wet nose against my fingers. Then he started to purr. He meowed again, as if to say, "What took you so long to get here?"

I barely remember the rest. Holmes filled out the paperwork and paid the ten dollar fee. Of course, I promised to pay him back. Then the lady got Ming out of his cage and put him in my arms. I didn't let go the whole way home.

As I sat in the back of the car with my friends, I cradled Ming in my arms and kissed his fuzzy forehead. He seemed perfectly happy just to cuddle up close to me.

Daisy and Hannah took turns petting him, and Ming thanked each of them with a meow. Daisy pulled the diamond collar from her pocket and put it on his neck. We now understood that the "M" stood for Ming, and not for Melvinia.

With his collar on, I have to say, I've never seen a cat look more beautiful. But I think I'll keep his diamond collar for special occasions only, since he'd already lost it once in the secret passageway. I didn't want him to lose that valuable collar again.

On the way home, we drove through the older part of Pinecrest. I wondered what it must have looked like when Aunt Melvinia and Archie were younger.

"Look!" Hannah pointed out the window. "That

building, right there! It's Archie's Diner."

Daisy and I turned our heads to see. She was right. It was Archie's Diner, even though the sign on top now said the "Graylight Grill." But it didn't matter. I would recognize that building anywhere. I knew it was really the diner that Aunt Melvinia had built and named in honor of her husband, Archie. I also knew it was the place where she fed lots of hungry people, who couldn't afford to pay her.

I had one other question that still stirred in my mind. I looked at Daisy and Hannah. "What was the gift that Archie wrote about in his last letter to Aunt Melvinia?"

"It must have been the tea set," Daisy said.

"It's a very nice set," Hannah added. "I'll bet Aunt Melvinia thought it was a wonderful present. But it looks like she never even took it out of the box. She probably was too heartbroken to use it after she heard that Archie wasn't coming home."

"You're probably right," I answered.

Then, for a few seconds, we were all quiet. I guess we were lost in thoughts of Aunt Melvinia and Archie.

Holmes pulled in our driveway and parked the car. Then he opened the door to let us out. Hannah and Daisy and I walked up the steps, smiling and petting Ming. He kept on purring and meowing, as though he was right at home.

Then, halfway up the steps, I suddenly realized there was just one little, itsy-bitsy, minor detail I had forgotten about. Holy Cannoli! I had forgotten my mom said I couldn't have a cat. Not unless I kept my room clean.

But I wasn't about to give up easily. Not after all we had been through today. Not after what it took for us to find him. I took a deep breath and climbed the rest of the steps with my friends. I held Ming tightly. We had one more obstacle to face, and I wasn't going to quit fighting now.

My mom was in the kitchen, and I didn't like the look on her face when she saw I had a cat. She actually looked kind of mad.

I stopped in the middle of the floor and Daisy and Hannah stood beside me. I guess this was one of those times when it really pays to have your friends with you.

"Look," I started, before my mom had a chance to speak. "Please let me explain about this cat before you say 'no.'"

My mom folded her arms in front of her and leaned against the counter. "Fair enough. I'm listening."

Okay, so far, so good. But the pressure was on. I had to convince my mom to let me keep Ming, no matter what. I couldn't let Ming go back to the animal shelter. I had to take care of him for Aunt Melvinia.

My heart began to beat loudly inside my chest. But it didn't matter. I stood up tall, took a deep breath and looked right at my mom. "First of all, this isn't just any cat, this was Aunt Melvinia's cat, Ming. You and dad said I could have any one item from Aunt Melvinia's house. And this is the one item I want. I want Ming."

Before I could go on, Hannah jumped in. "The

cat was Aunt Melvinia's most prize possession. He was so important to her." She started to bounce up and down.

"Now, how do you know that?" My mom asked.

Like a dam bursting, Hannah told the whole story of how we found Ming. She talked so fast that I could hardly keep up with her. She told my mom about how we found the note and read it with the WREB. She talked about how we thought Ming was a piece of old pottery at first. Then she told all we had learned about Aunt Melvinia and Archie. And so on and so on and so on.

Wowser! I've never heard Hannah talk so fast before. She told my mom everything about our afternoon.

The whole time, my mom didn't say a word. But I noticed her eyes went really wide when Hannah got to the part about how Sloan Snodgrass and Eddie wanted to kidnap us.

When Hannah finished talking, my mom didn't look mad anymore. In fact, she looked like she was trying not to smile.

Daisy took a step forward. "Mrs. Sosmart, didn't you say that Sally could have a cat if she kept her room clean?"

My mom nodded. "Yes, I did. But so far, she hasn't kept her room clean at all."

"But what if she agreed to keep her room clean from now on?" Daisy asked. "And what if Hannah and I helped her get it cleaned up today?"

That's when my mom finally broke into a smile. "All right, Daisy. I'd say you've got a deal. And I'd also say Sally is one very lucky girl to have friends like you and Hannah."

Now a smile broke out across my face. "Can I keep Ming, Mom? Do you mean it?"

My mom laughed. "Yes, Sally. You can keep Ming. But only if you hold up your end of the bargain and keep your room clean."

"I will, Mom! I promise!"

Then my mom gave us all hugs, and she even kissed Ming on the top of his shiny black head. "Welcome to the family," my mom said to Ming.

He meowed back to her like he was saying thanks.

"Thanks, Mom!" I said.

She picked up the phone and started to punch in some numbers. "I'd like you to go upstairs and get Ming settled in," she said. "Your friends are welcome to join us for dinner. But first I've got to talk to Detective Tom and report Sloan Snodgrass and his friend."

"Okay, Mom!" I hollered as I led Daisy and Hannah from the kitchen.

My friends and I ran to my room. I held Ming tightly all the way.

From that moment on, I vowed to keep my room clean forever. After all, I had to keep it clean so I could keep Ming. And I intended to take very good care of that cat.

Holy Cannoli! I had to. For me, for Ming, and most of all, for Aunt Melvinia.

About the Author

Cindy Vincent was born in Calgary, Alberta, and has lived all around the US and Canada. She is the award-winning author of the Mysteries by Vincent murder mystery party games and co-owner of the company. She lives with her husband and an assortment of perfectly pampered pets.

The Mystery

of the

Missing Ming